Teapots

The Fifth Husband

A Trilogy:

Book 1

Gabi Plumm

Teapots: The Fifth Husband

ASIN : B08J74JDCY – Kindle
ISBN: 9798689297064
Imprint: Independently published

This is a work of fiction and any references to historical events, real places are used fictitiously.
Names, characters and some places are products of the author's imagination.

Published by Gabi Plumm
2020.

This book is dedicated by all the elderly people I know who have been partnerless for a long time and are still longing for companionship. The friendship of those who care for you is priceless. Perhaps this little book will put a smile on your faces and even some hope in your hearts. You never know what's around the corner.

Thank you and I hope you enjoy my little tale!
Gabi Plumm

Contents

Chapter 1

'While there is tea, there is hope.'
Sir Arthur Pinero

The tilt train thundered north through the dry, boring landscape of the Townsville suburbs towards the winter balm of Cairns. The journey was no worse than he'd expected. A cup of tea in the restaurant car settled his nerves, although why he should be nervous about yet another life-change, he didn't know. Apprehensive, he thought, not so much nervous as apprehensive. But a life-change at his age was always going to be hard; not his idea, but he'd given in.

The Toyota Prius taxi hired at Cairns Station transported him and his two ancient leather suitcases through the back blocks of Cairns, past the malodorous transfer station, up the winding backstreets, through thick rainforest still dripping from the previous night's downpour, to dump him at the last place on earth he wanted to be.

"Staying for long then?" The driver waggled his bushy eyebrows.

"No."

"I bring a lot of people up here you know. Relatives mostly. Sometimes residents when they go to the shops and that. It's a nice place, so I'm told."

"Hmm."

"They're all old dears — you'll be popular I reckon, good

looking bloke like you. They'll be all over you like mushrooms on a dung heap."

Frank narrowed his eyes at the driver from behind his *Sculpture Today* journal, surprised at the attempt to be funny. Nothing felt remotely funny for him at that moment.

The rambling old Queenslander appeared from around a tight corner at the end of the gravel driveway. It was a pale pink, wooden building constructed around the middle of the 20th century; renovated, refurbished, and added to again. To Frank it looked like a set from a horror film. The magenta and orange bougainvillea that clung to the white newel posts flanking the front entrance did nothing to improve the gloom of the house, or appease his mood. He hated bougainvillea. He hated roses too, and although roses wouldn't grow at this tropical latitude. Even the Home's name made him shudder: Rosehill Retirement Home for Gentlefolk.

The driver hauled Frank's cases from the boot and dropped them unceremoniously on the forecourt. Frank gave him a fifty-dollar note and peered up at the faded façade.

"Keep the change," he said.

Noses peeked from behind white Colonial-style windows, but withdrew the instant they were spotted.

"Enjoy!" The driver tooted the horn as the gravel crunched beneath his wheels.

***

Dulcie, Dottie and Dierdre, fondly known as The Teapots by the staff and other residents of Rosehill, lounged in their Laziboys just inside the verandah doors. The evening rays of winter sunshine swept eager fingers over rows of handkerchief bushes in the gardens beyond. Creamy petals glowed like gold-dusted tissues; the spectacle at that time of day was not to be missed. The staff of the home had named the three ladies The Teapots because of their generously-proportioned figures, warm personalities and endless imbibing of Earl Grey tea.

In company with the Rolling Stones, the Teapots boasted 230 years between them. They'd been at the Home for five years, give or take a few months; placed in that haven of happiness by over-worked offspring who had no time for more than a quarterly visit — the guilt trips they called them.

A ruckus at the reception desk caused Dulcie to turn her head; a tricky maneuver with her neck encased in a soft brace. Tennis could be perilous at 71.

"I hope my room isn't one of those with roses all over it. I saw those in your brochure and I specifically requested plain walls." A warm but irritated baritone voice assaulted the ears of the receptionist, Madge Collins. She was used to it.

"I'm sorry, Mr Chambers, but you did tick the box for any room we had and we only have one available. And, yes, there is a very attractive wallpaper in that room." Madge kept her voice low so as not to disturb the recumbent residents, tummies full of lunch, slumbering in their loungers with newspapers or shawls over their heads.

"Well, I won't accept it. Anyway, my son ticked the box, not me. If I don't like it you'll just have to redecorate it."

"We'll do everything we can to make it work for you, Mr Chambers, but it won't be today — or tomorrow for that matter."

Dulcie tittered. "He'll be lucky!"

"What! What!" Dierdre — Dee to her teapot buddies — was buried under the enormous headphones her daughter Emilia had bought for her so she could listen to her iPod without annoying the other residents. Dee loved classical music having been a concert pianist in her youth, and she enjoyed the odd burst on the old upright piano that sat at the back of the lounge. She'd taken to wearing the headphones all the time so she didn't have to listen to other peoples' prattling. She'd spotted Dulcie's shoulders jiggling — not something that happened often in their Home for Gentlefolk.

"Nothing, Deeds. A new bloke's arrived and he doesn't want Mavis's old room. Thinks they'll redecorate it for him."

"Hah! Some hope of that. If he doesn't like roses he shouldn't have come here, they're bloody everywhere — 'cept in the garden, o' course." She went back to her iPod.

Dulcie placed her paperback carefully on the arm of her pink Laziboy, shifting her weight silently on the chair so she could study the new arrival. Tall and lean, broad shoulders somewhat a-stoop under a brown overcoat, his hair a tonsured grey, soft curls drizzling over his shirt collar — lazy or artistic, she wondered.

"Can someone take my cases to the room then? There's another one outside. I don't have to cart them up by myself, do I?" Frank wasn't prepared to be easy. He would find any excuse to go home.

Madge shook her head. "Of course not, sir. That won't be a problem. Once we have you settled — tomorrow — Dr Prince will come to your room and go through our orientation process." Madge made a sign at a young lad hanging around the front door, and he trotted out to the forecourt.

"Bloody orientation, sounds like the army. Sure I could manage."

Michael, Frank's son, had insisted on sending him away after Beryl died, and Rosehill had been the only retirement home with a vacancy. Michael believed that his father wouldn't be able to cope by himself. Anybody would think you were half dead once you'd reached your seventies. Nonsense, of course! He'd been able to look after Beryl in her last years; he knew he'd be fine on his own. But Michael wanted the house for himself, his wife and their little ones — their thirty-five-year-old family home — and the only way to get it was to park Frank somewhere else.

"It's just a formality to familiarise you with Rosehill, the garden, and our rules of engagement," said Madge, thinking the army reference might amuse him, but she shut her mouth when she saw Frank's expression. In pain, perhaps, she thought. "It won't take long and Dr Prince will do your medical checks at the same time. All the things that everyone does when they first come here. Quite normal." Madge offered a lopsided smile in the hope that he might relax and appreciate her courteous welcome. She handed him a piece of paper and a key. "Here we go, a little mud map to help you find your way around. We'll see you at six then, not long now — dinner time — in the dining room."

After many years of checking elderly folk into the home, Madge was accustomed to their reluctance; they were always unhappy, nobody wanted to be offloaded by their children. Mr Chambers was no exception.

Timmy, the young porter, arrived with the second suitcase, and nodding at Mr Chambers they headed for the lift.

Dulcie, hips, shoulders and head suitably angled to watch the show, gave a start as Frank Chambers turned from the reception desk to follow Timmy. A long dormant sensation flashed through her body like a skewer in her heart. She shuddered and scratched her nose, before maneuvering herself back to take in the evening view— such a beautiful view — and smile at her busy friends: Dottie clicking away with her knitting needles and Dierdre humming along with Mr Beethoven.

***

Frank didn't want any dinner, he had to get unpacked first anyway. Right now he had to handle the problem in front of him: a rose-papered bedroom. Almost his worst nightmare. Timmy led the way along the dark, musty corridor to Frank's room and unlocked the door. He kept the door open as he dropped Frank's two cases on the dark green carpet, and Frank had his first view of his next prison. No.23. Frank thanked Timmy, slipping a $5 note into his hand, then closed the door behind him. He wanted to keep his eyes shut but knew he would have to see it sooner or later. His heart was pounding in his throat when he glanced around the rose-papered room. Why did it still affect him so? He didn't know. He just knew this was worse than he could have ever imagined; roses everywhere, even on the bloody ceiling, plasterwork in the shape of a huge ceiling rose, picked out in three different pinks. Dear God, how could he avoid seeing it? Maybe if he pretended he was blind and just felt his way around the room? Maybe he could paint over it when no one was looking; he would consider that if it looked like he couldn't escape. Eyes lowered, he opened his suitcases, and removed his personal items one by one, rehousing them on the shelves that formed part of a wardrobe unit.

Beside the wardrobe sat a large, silky-oak tallboy. Into its drawers he neatly placed his singlets, socks and underwear. Trousers and shirts were distributed to the plentiful hangers in the cupboard. A small bag of potpourri was hanging around the hook of one of the padded ones, and as he reached in to withdraw it the bag broke, and dried rose-petals confettied onto the carpet. Frank clamped his hand over his nose, and turned his head so fast his neck crunched. The pain shot to the top of his skull and he dropped his trousers, clamping his other hand onto the nape. Two paces took him to the casement window. He pushed it open as far as it would go, breathing deep to clear his nose of the hated fragrance. His heart galloped while he hyperventilated, his knuckles white on the windowsill. When the panic subsided, he laid his forehead on his hands and squeezed his eyes shut to stop the tears from dribbling down his cheeks. He was astonished it still had that effect on him. It must be the accumulation of the day's stress: saying goodbye to his son and the family home, to his wife's grave, and travelling 450 kilometres to this rose-papered hell. How would he ever be able to endure it? Hadn't those war hospitals been enough? He turned from the window, and pain shot northward again bringing him to his knees. He crawled to the bed, squashed a pillow under his neck and closed his eyes.

Dinner was a sedate affair at Rosehill. There was never much joy to be seen on the faces of the world-weary residents. Many of the less mobile took meals in their rooms, so on this beautiful autumn evening only ten of the usual thirteen were present when the new bloke entered, fingers jangling the room key in his jacket pocket.

Frank had allowed himself an hour's sleep, but his neck was still sore even after a hot shower, followed by 30 seconds under the cold tap; a routine he had followed for so many years he couldn't remember when it had started. The change in water temperature had always fortified his constitution, and in his younger days, cold showers were often all that were available. Yet his neck had been an ever-nagging problem since falling from a horse at the age of 12. He'd undergone countless massages, physiotherapy sessions and chiropractic for only marginal relief, and the older he got the more likely it was to play up when new circumstances meant strange beds, and stress lifted his shoulders up around his ears. He wished he could have simply stayed asleep until the morning but it wasn't to be, so he dragged himself down to the dining room to face yet another set of new faces.

If he was disappointed at not finding his name on a place setting at any of the three prepared tables, he hid it well. The dining room resembled every institutional dining room he'd ever seen, except, admittedly, it wasn't painted government green, but a soft pink with a dado of red and white roses ringing the room at waist level. Tables all the same: round, white, melamine, covered in white plastic tablecloths, accommodating a trio of groups. At one there were three large ladies involved in either knitting, reading or listening to something through enormous headphones, one with two gentlemen and two ladies, partnered pairs perhaps, and a third with two ladies flanking a tiny, hunched, bespectacled man who resembled a vulture with his bald head bent over a half-empty plate. Frank made for that one. The man squinted up at him through coke-bottle specs, one of the ladies looked trout-mouthed at him as he approached, but the third, a vast amazon of a woman with a vivid orange afro, jerked to her feet as he neared the table. The hair-do made her almost as tall as him, her smile full of brown-gapped teeth seemed predatory, and Frank recoiled.

"Here! Here! Come over here!" the woman helloed, rubbing her palms together. "Sit, please. Sit with us. I'm Joan, but you can call me Joanie." Frank did as he was bid, smiling tentatively at the only one of the three who'd acknowledged him. "You must be the new bloke. Aren't you the handsome one then!" Joanie patted Frank's knee once he was seated, but he whipped it away as if burnt. "I'm the longest-surviving resident of Rosehill, so there's nothing I can't tell you about this place. This is Samuel, he doesn't talk much." She pointed to the bald pate. "And this is Prudence. Prudence, say hello. This is — I'm sorry I didn't catch your name!"

"I'm Frank, Frank Chambers. I just arrived this afternoon. Only just checked in." He grabbed a white serviette and spread it across his knees.

One table away the three ladies glanced at each other. Dulcie twitched. She tried to turn around as she had her back to Joan's table, but the brace made it impossible, and she didn't want to make a loud noise by scraping the chair on the tiled floor.

"Dot, change places with me," she whispered, "quickly."

"Why, I'm quite happy here. What's the matter with you, Dulcie?"

"Ssh. I just want to … oh never mind."

The partnered pairs gave cursory glances at the newcomer and shrugged their shoulders; they'd seen Joan in action before. They continued pushing ham, salad and tiny, tinned potatoes around their plates.

A uniformed girl appeared through a swing door carrying a plate of food and placed it in front of Mr. Chambers, who nodded his appreciation, then peered at his salad.

"What does he look like? Dee! Can you hear me? Take those

things off your ears. What does he look like?"

"Who?"

"For goodness sake — the new bloke. Dot, can you see him? What does he look like?"

"Looks like an old bloke, Dulce, that's all. What do you want him to look like, Rock Hudson?"

Dulcie gritted her teeth. Undeterred, she rose from her chair, untangled the bamboo cane that was hanging over the back, and tapped her way through the empty tables towards the Toilets.

"Where're you going?"

"Just to the la-ta, Dee. If that's alright with you!"

Dulcie hobbled into the alcove by the toilets, and poked her head out from around the corner. She could almost see the newcomer from there. She wiped a smear of mayonnaise from her glasses with the tail of her blouse and peered at him again.

He didn't look familiar from behind, but he looked to be almost bald, so it was hardly surprising; she didn't know many bald men other than the ones already resident at Rosehill. Frank Chambers, that's what he'd said. Couldn't be her Frank Chambers, he was dead. And he'd never been bald. But it had been fifty years since she'd seen him. She'd never forgotten the name, or the nose. She peered through the mayonnaise-smudged specs at his back. She couldn't see his nose, or his face for that matter. And she well knew that faces and noses change over the years; faces droop and noses get bigger. Couldn't be him. Just the same name. Her heart did a flip of disappointment tinged with relief. She never wanted to go through that again. Dulcie fiddled with the coloured beads hanging, rosary-like over her bosom, while she watched Joan's seduction routine. She hoped to God it wasn't her Frank. Joanie's attentions were a fate worse than death.

She heaved a big huff and hooked the cane over her arm so she could push the bathroom door open with both hands. A small puddle of something sticky outside the door grabbed at her slippers, and she snatched at the handle to stop herself from toppling. The cane skittered onto the floor as she fought for balance. She closed her eyes, and pressed her hand to her chest, hoping that no one had been attracted by the clatter — they were all so deaf they probably wouldn't hear anyway. She stooped for the cane and with heart galloping, pushed the la-ta door open.

The la-ta, as the Teapots called it, was empty; the stall doors hung open like a spent Christmas advent calendar. Dulcie peered at herself in the full-length mirror, then put her mayonnaise-smeared glasses back on; kinder on the elderly soul. Her salt and pepper hair, more salt than pepper these days, corkscrewed down her pale cheeks to rest on her shoulders. The fierce sun of the tropics might not be good for the skin, but a light toasting would be preferable to the pasty face that greeted her. She couldn't see her double chin for the neck brace but it wasn't as bad as Dottie's – she had three. Saggy round the gills perhaps, but not yet like a Sharpei. Her eyes, always her best feature, were still bright and periwinkle blue. Body wise she was a mess. Not buxom by any means but she'd become matronly, rotund with a few spare tyres. She prayed that the new bloke, the new Frank Chambers was not her Frank, she didn't know how she could face him if it was. There were not enough hiding places in Rosehill and one could only stay in one's bedroom for so long. The rose wallpaper would drive one insane after a couple of days. She splashed water over her make-up-less cheeks hoping it might erase the fifty years of wrinkles linocut into her face. I'm still the same person I was fifty years ago. It's only the picture in the mirror that's changed. She put the thought out of her mind; she simply would not think about it — pointless supposing or imagining when it was pure fancy. Her Frank was dead and buried, even if not in her heart. She had never gotten over her first love, destroyed, as it had been by her parents' disapproval and somebody else's war. She took one last ironic look, and left the la-ta to rejoin her friends in the dining-room.

"Where've you been, Dulce?" Dottie peered over her specs, her knitting lying abandoned on her empty ham and salad plate, a lone potato peeking out one side.

"Just to the la-ta, Dot. Didn't you want that potato?"

"Na, too much for me. I think they gave me yours anyway. They think I've put on too much weight. Here, you have it darlin', all yours!" she picked the potato up with a knitting needle and shook it onto Dulcie's plate.

"Anything exciting planned for tomorrow?" Dee asked, taking one headphone away from her ear.

"Tennis with John McEnroe at 10.30 followed by a three-course lunch of poached salmon and a tickly little Chablis with Jim Courier and Chrissie Evert." Dot giggled. "You?"

"Injury has stopped play in my case, as you can see," said Dulcie, stroking her neck-brace, "I shall have to deal with a little visit to Dr Prince's torture chamber at 10, then who knows what wonders the rest of the day may hold?"

Dee chuckled, hooked her headphones around her neck, grabbed her iPod and handbag and pushed her chair back.

"I'm done, darlings, see you mañana!"

"Night night. See you on the 'morrow."

"Night night, darlin.' Another day in paradise!"

Chapter 2

'What would the world do without tea?...
I am glad I was not born before tea'.
Rev. Sydney Smith

The Teapots had been friends ever since coming to Rosehill. It wasn't a bad place compared to some they'd heard about. It was designed for the over fifty-fives who had money put by and wanted an easier life without the hassle of houses and mortgages; it was quite the rage when it first opened. It also suited their kids who moved into huge family homes and thus took on the financial burden. Logical they said. Most of the residents had been there since their late sixties and were now creeping up the ladder into the eighties' attic.

The garden was beautiful: ten acres of carefully tended tropical maze in the rain-forested hills behind Cairns, Far North Queensland. It was warrened with pathways and secret nooks around every corner. Many a resident had become lost in its wonder at one time or another. And not just lost in its wonder but actually lost for a day or two. It was after all, a maze. Many was the time the Ambos had been called in from Cairns Base along with the Firies with their hoses and high powered torches and megaphones, calling and hollering through the hallowed hedges of Rosehill Maze. Some even thought that a missing pensioner was an intended amusement, it created magnificent drama and chatter along the sunset veranda; some even thought there was a roster. When life became unbearably dull, a bejeweled finger would point dramatically at the owner of the next name on the list. The target's pockets would be surreptitiously stuffed with dates, bananas and water bottles and sent on their way. But this was just a rumour. No one knew who kept the list, or if it even existed.

There were two couples: the Smithsons and the Stillwells. They enjoyed their own suite of rooms: bigger bedrooms with lounges and small dinettes along with ensuite bathrooms. Each suite was at the opposite end of the house, so any wife swapping would have been hindered by midnight travelling distance as the house spanned almost half a kilometre from end to end. Whoever thought that wife-swapping was a possibility for couples in their late 70s was either still in their 40s or had been watching some very peculiar movies.

The other possibility was that Joanie, Joan Holloway-Potts-Jones, the major shareholder of Rosehill, had insisted that couples should have their own space, not just their own suite of rooms but half the upper corridor to themselves. Her room was one such room (there were three) and she had always imagined that one day a newcomer would appear who would become her perfect 'other,' her knight in shining armour to sweep her off her feet and carry her off to her spacious boudoir where they could make as much noise as they wished without the singleton hoy polloi listening in.

All the other residents had their own rose-papered bedroom and bathroom on the first floor; mostly pink but there were three blue ones. Samuel had one, Mike Partridge and Dave Meldrum, the other two lone wolves, had the others and now, the latest arrival, Frank Chambers, had a recently vacated pink one. What he wouldn't give to have one of the blue ones, or one with nothing on the walls at all.

***

Dulcie's appointment the next morning with Dr Prince was to remove her neck brace. She didn't think he would allow her back on the tennis court until she'd done a few exercises to strengthen it; swimming perhaps. At least they had a decent pool at Rosehill even though it was a bit chilly at this time of year. She chuckled, tennis court my backside! A small line-painted quadrangle where one tottered about with little plastic paddles and large squishy balls, that's all they had. She liked to call it a half court; she'd been pretty good in her day. She sat patiently in the waiting room and flicked through a Woman's Day magazine.

The door beside her opened and a tall man entered. Dressed in pressed khaki shorts and a plain blue collared shirt, his shoulder length grey curls belied his military bearing. His head was cocked strangely to one side; he looked to be in pain. Dulcie stopped breathing and tightened her fingers around the magazine. She dropped her head onto her chest, her heart drumming in her throat like a tattoo. He was walking away from her towards the desk; he wouldn't see her as long as he didn't turn round. She scolded herself for being such an idiot. This man couldn't be Frank. Her Frank was long gone, but maybe just the likeness was giving her palpitations.

The consulting room door opened and Dr Prince called, "Mrs Dooley, come on through, let's get that brace off, shall we."

Dulcie grabbed her cane, heaved herself from the bucket chair and hobbled into the doctor's room. She half turned to look at the man, but he was deep in conversation with Pamela, the surgery receptionist. She closed the door behind her.

By the time Dulcie left the surgery she was breathing easier. Once the brace was off she escaped to her bedroom, chuckling at her girlish folly, and the thought of the other teapots playing tennis with John McEnroe. Not! She'd been relieved that the man wasn't in the waiting room when she'd emerged from Dr Prince's rooms, but even that, she knew, was silly. It was inevitable that she would meet him at some time, and then she would see that he was just a Frank Chambers lookalike. Nothing to get het up about at all.

The kettle on her little kitchen benchtop hummed and she filled her teapot. She pondered the paleness of the water as it trickled into her teacup. She'd forgotten to put the tea bag in! She muttered to herself and plopped the Earl Grey sachet into the cup. A splash of milk and a spoonful of sugar completed the job. She set the cup on the side table next to her chair, which received her kilos with kindness. She plucked a ginger nut from the biscuit box on the table and lifted the cup to her lips.

A photo of her family in a silver frame reminded her of the life she'd had before coming to Rosehill. A sip of tea brought memories bubbling to the surface. She knew she should avoid them; it was a pointless exercise only filled with pain and sadness. And for what? She looked longingly at the photo of her daughter, Stella, and wondered when she would visit again. It had been a while.

Dulcie gave a mighty snort, jerked her recently-freed head back and felt a twang in her neck. To be expected, Dr Prince had said, the little cracking sounds were only Nitrogen bubbles popping. But Dulcie had been elsewhere for a while and her tea had gone cold and dribbled into the saucer. Her cheeks were wet and her nose a little drippy. She put the cup back on the side table and heaved herself out of the chair to pull a tissue from a rose-patterned box. She looked at herself in the mirror above the kettle, and saw fifty years of sorrow red-rimming her eyes, her small double chin wobbling with the quivering of her lower lip. She snatched another handful of tissues and blew her nose. She slumped on to her bedcover, pink roses and green leaves drooping over the edge, and she wept. For what, she didn't really know. This newcomer, this Frank lookalike had awakened memories she'd long buried, and she wanted to keep them there, but the tears had other ideas.

***

A love of art had brought Frank and Dulcie together when, at 21, she'd changed tack at the University of Queensland in Brisbane. She came from a wealthy family of lawyers and doctors, and had given in to their insistence that she should train to be a solicitor. She'd completed two years of mind-numbing study. The idea of three more years of torture for what she considered to be the dullest of occupations was sufficient to drive her to drink. Or, look for another option. A girlfriend suggested switching to a Fine Arts degree and Dulcie jumped at it. Her parents had not been so keen. They hadn't tried to hide their disappointment when she told them she was changing her major. She'd always loved painting at school. She didn't want to be a lawyer; she wanted to be an artist.

One Saturday morning at a gallery in the Queen Street Mall, she was backing away from an impressionist painting to get a better perspective, when her stiletto heel punctured the back of a moccasin worn by a curly-haired young man who'd been leaning over a sculpture behind her. She whirled round to apologise; he did the same. They laughed and said sorry at the same time. The ensuing cup of tea in the Sorrento Café on Anne Street established beyond doubt that she was in love. She couldn't take her eyes off him; and it was mutual.

Frank's Italian heritage had blessed him with dark brown eyes, olive skin and an astonishing smile that had melted Dulcie's heart from the beginning. He'd been christened Franco Cambiarini in Venice. For no obvious reason, his parents had changed their last name to Chambers upon arrival in Australia, and Franco had evolved into Frank. His desire to be a sculptor instigated his enrollment into the Fine Arts program at the University of Queensland. When he met Dulcie, he was 24 years old and in his third year, having spent two years in Europe visiting every gallery he could find. He was two years ahead of Dulcie, and surrounded by young women eager to become Mrs Chambers. So far he'd resisted them all and after his first meeting with Dulcie he was glad he had.

Dulcie's parents made no secret of their disapproval of her relationship with Frank because, first and foremost he was foreign, and adding insult to injury, he was an artist. They'd done everything they could to separate them, but failing to win with threats of expulsion from the family, they'd cut her off without a penny forcing her to get a menial job and to take a room in University Hall. This only made her more determined to be with Frank, and this she did with relish.

His lodgings on the third floor of a semi-detached house in St Lucia consisted of the tiniest of bedsitting rooms. To call it a bedsitting room was asking a lot of the imagination; there wasn't enough room for the bed let alone a sitting room. The cramped accommodation included a kitchenette in one corner, and a minuscule shower room, toilet and basin in the other. Comfortable it wasn't, but their love made them blind to the things that others might have called squalid.

It was only a couple of months before physical compulsion took their relationship to a deeper level; to be apart was too painful to contemplate. Dulcie moved in with Frank and they made the most of every day and night to the exclusion of friends, and their studies. Their love was so all-consuming that they were unaware of the threat of the 1964 Conscription Birthday Ballot, and Dulcie's missing period.

***

Dulcie sobbed into her handful of tissues as she remembered the glory of the baby girl who'd arrived eight months after Frank had left for Vietnam, for the agony as his train pulled out of the station heading for Sydney and Saigon. She thought of the ring she'd worn for years on her engagement finger, a ring he would never match with its wedding partner. She thought he would die out there having never seen his baby girl, having never even known there was one, having never become the brilliant sculptor he was destined to be, and having doomed her to single parenthood and penury until Bob Dooley came along and loved her enough to raise another man's child. Her parents had disowned her. She'd never heard from Frank again; no letters, nothing, and she knew he was gone forever.

Chapter 3

'Each cup of tea represents an imaginary voyage.'
Catherine Douzel

The autumn day was very warm and humid, but the air-conditioning was cool as Frank made his way to the dining room to check out the seating arrangements in daylight. He thought if he got there early he could avoid another meeting with the orangutan — his name for Joan —with her orange afro and long arms; a reach he would rather avoid. He would find a seat with the other chaps and make some friends. It looked different in the daylight. The paintwork, pink of course, was fresh and clean and the melamine tables and padded chairs seemed new. A large, modern stainless steel and glass servery lined one wall. An alcove with Exit and Toilets signs led off the left corner with a kitchen swing door at the other end. A pale tiled floor with a long maroon stripe down the centre drew the residents from the lounge into the dining room as if they needed a path to follow to get them to their food or away from it. He looked back to the reception desk where he'd been admitted the night before. The staircase up to the bedrooms led from the hallway beside the lift, but he'd gone out the back door that morning to the doctor's surgery and bypassed the breakfasting residents.

Dr Prince had examined his neck, bade him lie on the couch, massaged and manipulated the vertebrae until they hurt no more and told Frank to be gentle with himself for a while; no acrobatics, no swinging from chandeliers. The doctor had chuckled at his little joke, but he knew what the ladies were like in this place; he wouldn't put it past any of them.

Frank liked the doctor immediately. He was a couple of inches shorter than Frank with a jolly round face and a full mane of iron-grey hair. His hazel eyes had sparkled when he spoke about the residents. He obviously had a genuine caring for them. He'd recognised that Frank had all his marbles in the right places, and had carried out the standard checks without much ado.

"Sorry about the formalities, Mr Chambers, we do need to make sure everyone knows the rules. Some are very skilled at breaking them, but you need to know them first of course. Ha! Ha!" Dr Prince knew what the old codgers got up to.

"I understand. Don't worry, I'm not about to go diving into the pool from the highest board, or plunge into a lake full of crocodiles."

"Oh, it's not that so much as the sneaking about at night into other people's rooms. Sometimes it's by mistake, but mostly it isn't. It's a rule of the house to stay in your own area. You'd be surprised what they get up to."

"No problem. I'm hoping not to be here too long anyway. My son, Michael, will be coming to get me soon — I hope."

"Good. Lunch at 12 then. You know where I am if you need any painkillers for that neck. Take care now." Dr Prince ushered Frank out the door.

Frank checked the dining room again, and identified a place to sit when lunchtime came. He left the building by the veranda door, and set off at a good pace to explore the grounds; work up an appetite. He waved politely to the group of ladies who were lounging on Laziboys under umbrellas on the verandah in front of the sitting room. The same three he'd seen in the dining room the night before. One had her nose in a book, one was knitting like fury, and the third appeared to be humming, head phones plugged in. Nice, he thought. Three old ducks in a row.

The gravel pathway meandered between some high, glossy-leaved plants; pale creamy flowers in languid droop reminded him of the handkerchief bushes he'd grown in his garden in Townsville. Those flowers had been pink, but he imagined these to be of a similar ilk. He caressed them as he passed and a downy dust floated to the ground. Once around the corner the trees all but hid the ugly bougainvillea-smothered house, and he breathed a sigh of relief. No bloody roses here at least. Thank God for small mercies.

***

Dulcie had seen him appear at the veranda entrance, and had quickly buried her nose in her book.

"Book's upside down, Dulce. You won't get much read like that, darlin'!" Dottie chuckled. "There's that bloke you were looking at yesterday. Gone for a walk. He just waved at us. Maybe he fancies Dierdre! What do you think, Deeds? Oi, Dee, DEE. Bloody hell there could be a war going on and she'd never know."

Dulcie started; mention of war always did that to her, even now.

"Hey, Dulce, how's your neck? Looks better with the torture cuff off."

"Oh yes, much better thanks, Dot. Feel free again. Ready to take on the world. Dr Prince says it'll be a week before I can get back on the court though. Have to make do with ping-pong." They chuckled.

Dulcie peered down the length of the lawn and into the bushes as she spoke. Once again she'd only seen his back as he was striding away. She wished she could get more involved in her book, *Anna Karenina,* but it was hard going at the beginning, and she imagined herself swapping it for something more gripping, a thriller crime suspense thing, perhaps. She decided to head back to the Library later that day, or tomorrow, no hurry. She had to take her mind off this man who had got her head in a spin for no reason at all. She knew that the minute she saw his face, that he would have a small nose, blue eyes and thin lips … nothing like her Frank at all. She felt silly and irritable but her heart was still bounding about. Maybe she'd have a heart attack and never know any more about it, or him, or anything.

***

Frank wandered through the garden maze. The energy of the tropical plants and the warmth of the sun were relaxing him. He almost felt happy, maybe he would be happy if he could forget the reasons for him being here. After half an hour he looked at his watch. 11.50. He should be getting back; time for lunch.

He turned and followed the gravel path beside some hibiscus bushes, pink and red in glorious profusion, meeting a fork after only twenty paces. Which way had he come? He had no idea. Right or left? His heart banged a loud drum, once, twice and then again. I can't be lost, not already! He made a choice and took the right fork, noting the hibiscus he was leaving behind. He made a line in the gravel with his shoe and set off. Thirty paces later he came to another fork, and he lurched into the left branch leaving another smudge in the gravel. He looked up into the sky, searching for the sun. He carried on. Another fork. He took the left one again and made his mark. Poinsettia bushes lined the paths, their leaves high and red; Christmas coloured. He wasn't going to be stuck here until Christmas. He stopped and filled his lungs. Breathe — breathe. His heart was hammering in his chest, and he knew the signs of panic; he'd been there before, been lost in a jungle before. It hadn't ended well. This time it couldn't end anything but well; he was in a retirement home for God's sake not an Asian hornet's nest. The Poinsettias changed into handkerchief bushes, and the creamy flowers seemed to smile at him. Was he back? Was he at the end of this nightmare path? He ran. Around a corner, the building appeared; the hated bougainvillea-covered newel posts, welcoming. He pulled himself up at the end of the pathway, tugged his shirt down, smoothed his hair over his collar, scrubbed his face with both hands, and took a steadying breath.

He could see the residents at luncheon; someone had nabbed his intended place. He strode up the garden to the dining room entrance and surveyed the scene, hoping he didn't look as flushed as he felt.

Joan leapt to her feet. "Frank, Frank, over here. I saved a place for you." His heart plummeted but he pasted on a smile, and wound his way towards her from the veranda doors.

She pulled a chair out for him. "You look a little hot, dear." She fingered the hair on his arm where droplets of perspiration were still sitting on his skin. He pulled his arm away and wiped the moisture off with his free hand. He tried a smile. "Just went for a little walk. Nice jungle you have here."

"Ha! Ha!" Joan's raucous laugh made him start. He might change her nickname to Hyena, Orangutans never make that kind of noise. "Get lost did you? Everyone gets lost the first time. I'll take you for a tour later. Make sure you know the paths. You won't get lost again. There's ten acres of garden out there to explore. Won't that be fun?" She grinned and indicated the chair she'd prepared for him. Frank sat down. She poured some water from an ice-filled jug and passed him the tumbler. He nodded his thanks and drained the glass.

Dulcie heard the conversation behind her. She hadn't asked Dottie to change places, she didn't want to see this Frank person's face. She'd decided to avoid him altogether if possible, get a better book to read. She knew full well that the minute she actually saw his unfamiliar visage, she would be ridiculously disappointed. It couldn't possibly be him, she was just having elderly delusions. But, there was an element of drama and suspense in the not-knowing and part of her was actually enjoying it. She didn't want it to end. But now she was hearing Joan doing her claim-staking routine, she wanted to race to the poor man's rescue.

"That's the old bloke you were pretending not to be interested in, Dulce. Looks like he lost himself in the garden. Joan'll sort him out … you all right, Dulce?" Dottie put her knitting on her empty plate and narrowed her eyes at her friend.

Dierdre looked up at them both. "What! What's going on?"

Dottie pulled the headphones from Dee's ears. "If you didn't spend all day and night in your bloody iPod, Dierdre Minns, you might know what's going on. Joanie's boyfriend got lost in the garden, and now she's taking him in hand."

"Joanie's boyfriend? She got a new one then?"

"Oh, for Gawd's sake! The bloke who arrived yesterday — you know — the one Dulcie was sneaking around trying to get a peek at. Finger on the pulse, Deeds."

"Does she know 'im then?"

"No — 'course not — do you, Dulce?"

"It would be nice if you two would stop talking about me as if I wasn't here? I'm not dead you know. Of course, I don't know him. Wouldn't know him from a bar of soap. I'm going up for a rest. Had enough of today." Dulcie grabbed her cane and left the dining room at a brisk totter, leaving Dottie and Dierdre gawping after her.

Dulcie didn't know whether to laugh or cry. It was all too silly. Too daft. She bent over in the hallway near the reception desk to get her breath. That Joan! Poor man. She took some deep breaths and concentrated on getting her heart to settle down. She'd learnt how to do that in meditation classes and more often than not it worked. She wasn't so sure today.

She headed for the lift as soon as her heart had slowed a bit then glanced at a worried-looking Madge behind the reception desk.

"Are you all right, Mrs Dooley?"

"Oh Madge, yes I'm fine, just a bit too much laughter at lunch makes me a bit giddy. I'm going upstairs for a little nap. Might even take my dinner in my room tonight, would that be all right? Would you like me to phone down to the kitchen?"

"No, don't you worry, I'll take care of it. They'll send a plate of you know what up at 6pm."

"Ham, salad and tiny, tinned potatoes?" she chuckled. "Thank you, Madge, that would be kind."

Dulcie pushed the up-button for the lift. It tinged almost immediately and she tottered in, her cane tapping on the linoleum floor. The doors closed and it started its laborious ascent.

***

Frank managed to escape after half an hour of agonizing conversation with Joan. Prudence and Samuel had joined them after only ten minutes so he was spared the embarrassment of the long, lingering looks Joan was sending him across the table.

Sam peered up at Frank and scowled, while Prudence pulled his chair back from the table and pushed it back in after he'd sat down. Frank was bemused by what looked like a rather mismatched relationship particularly after Samuel sent daggers his way at Joan's simpering. Have to get away from this, he thought. Time to buddy up with some of the chaps. He had noticed two single gents at another table and determined to sit with them that night.

He made his apologies to Joan, Prudence and Samuel and headed for the lounge. Time to rest his neck and finish his unpacking.

One of the older ladies was tottering out of the lounge towards the reception and he saw her briefly chat to Madge. She wasn't bad, he thought. He'd been a bit abrupt with her the day before, an apology might be in order.

As he reached the desk the lift door closed and started its slow climb to the next floor. He would take the stairs.

"Hello, Miss Collins," said Frank, peering fleetingly at the badge on her ample bosom. "Just wanted to apologize for my rudeness yesterday. Had a long, hot journey, not a nice situation. But no excuse for rudeness."

"No apology necessary, Mr Chambers. We're very familiar with the difficulties some of our residents encounter before coming to stay with us. And we will endeavor to change a few things in your room, if you're really unhappy with it." Madge patted Frank's hand. He gently drew it away.

"Yes, yes, that would be very good, even a coat of white paint would help. I have a horror of roses you see, old history … war stuff … difficult to talk about … nightmarish really."

Madge smiled and tucked her hands under the desk. "Totally understand, Mr Chambers. We'll get our handyman on to it, pronto."

He nodded his thanks again and headed for the stairs.

Chapter 4

'Strange how a teapot can represent at the same time,
the comforts of solitude and the pleasures of company.'
Anon

Dulcie threw her cane onto the bed and headed for the kettle. She poked around in her voluminous handbag for *Anna Karenina,* pulled tissues and reading glasses out ahead of the book and chucked them all onto the bed next to the cane. She switched the kettle on and pinched her fingers around an Earl Grey Tea bag which she popped into her rose-patterned teapot. There are times when I'm mighty fed up with roses, she thought as she scanned the room; the heavily patterned wallpaper echoing the pink and green floral display of the bedspread. She felt like screaming. If I wasn't 71 I'd think I was premenstrual. She giggled and the kettle hooted in unison.

Oh my good Gawd, she thought, what if I rather fancy this Frank lookalike? Turn him into a Frank replacement and have a bit of fun? Joanie's not the only one who can have a boyfriend, maybe he'll like me better. She shuddered. No way anyone would like her better than Joanie.

She filled the teapot with water, admired the proper colour, poured it into her cup with a dash of milk and some sugar, sat herself down in her big friendly chair, and looked longingly at the photo of her daughter in an ornate silver frame that her husband, Bob had given her before he passed away seven years ago.

As she sipped her tea her mind flashed back to the birth of her daughter, Stella. She'd called her Stella because when she was in labour she could see a late star out of her window in the early morning sky. It wasn't a closed ward in a hospital. She'd had her baby at her friend Patty's house with a midwife that Patty had paid for. She was lucky there had been no complications, she'd never even considered those possibilities at the time but knew very well now just how things could go wrong. She'd been lucky, if you could consider it lucky to have a baby out of wedlock, with no idea where the father was or if he was still alive. She'd had to move house so many times after Frank had left for the war she had wondered if his letters might have gone astray. But she believed that Australia Post, or The Royal Mail as it still was then, could have, should have caught up with her. All the bills did. No, Frank was dead, probably in an unmarked grave somewhere in the tropical forests of Vietnam. She should put her silly fancies away, get a decent book and go to bed early. It would all be different in the morning.

***

Frank let himself into his room, closing his eyes and groping his way to the window. He opened it wide again and leaned out. The view was truly lovely, he had to admit. The window overlooked the maze where he'd been lost that morning. The bushes and trees were stunning in their array of colours, so marvellous even in the autumn — the glory of the tropics.

He thought about Joan and wondered why she had hooked on to him, particularly as he would put money on the notion that little Samuel had a mighty crush on her. He chuckled. If those two ever got together she would be the crusher. She was an enormous woman, not his type at all. He missed Beryl, she had been his wife for a very long time and he had loved her. But Michael had been a bit tricky in the beginning. He was not Frank's child and was very much a mummy's boy even though they had eventually settled well as a family.

Frank sighed and approached the little kitchen bench where a kettle resided, flanked by milk jug and tea caddy, plus a small fridge, nestled under the bench. He unplugged the kettle and took it to a sink beside the counter top, filled it with water then switched it on. A little red light came on near the power lead and something about that normality gave him comfort. He left the kettle to do its thing and made for the bathroom.

After his shower, he inspected his body in the mirror, wondering what on earth a handsome woman like Joan could see in him. She was handsome for sure but her laugh would drive him nuts in no time. She was an Angelica Houston type, high and haughty. Perhaps she played the vamp with all new arrivals. Maybe the other chaps would know.

He peered at his body. He was still lean and his skin was saggy only around the scars. One long horizontal shark-bite type scar stitched across his belly where part of his colon had been removed through bowel cancel four years earlier. He was lucky they had caught it early. Under his collarbone was a furrow that a bullet had ploughed. That one would never fill in. The long scars on his legs were in line with his thighs so not much damage showed there, but the muscles in his arms had withered over the past two years; his wife's illness had kept him housebound and he'd been unable to exercise.

He'd regained his fitness after his discharge from the hospital in Townsville in 1976. His bones had healed well. His mind was another thing altogether, and he'd sought sanctuary as an art teacher in a suburban college. It was easy work, and although he'd never got his degree from the University of Queensland, he knew enough about art and sculpture to be able to teach the subject. He'd met Beryl in 1979. She was a pretty little Irish redhead who had trained as a nurse. She had a two-year-old son, Michael. His father had been a one-month wonder who had breezed into Beryl's life, taken her virginity, neglecting to mention that he was married to someone else; someone whose newborn baby he had also fathered. He'd left Beryl without knowing she was pregnant. She'd never told him, preferring to muddle through on her own. She adored little Michael, a blond, laughing monkey of a child who soon endeared himself to Frank.

Even in the 80s, attitudes in Queensland were such that unmarried mothers, medical training or not, would have difficulty getting work. Frank hadn't fallen in love with Beryl but they had enough in common for him to marry her and take on the fatherhood of little Michael. She had quickly become devoted to Frank, happy to help in his mental and physical rehabilitation. For Frank, the woman he'd lost because of an unfortunate birth date had never relinquished her number one spot in his heart. He would never forget her, but having never received any response to his letters, he assumed she was either dead, or her life had turned out well, and he'd decided to leave the past in the past.

His eleven months in the army hospital near Townsville had involved numerous operations on broken limbs; two compound fractures of his femurs from shrapnel and gunfire. Nightmares plagued his sleep — images of scarlet petals that bloomed in the chests of his dying comrades. The dreams of the hungry red 'roses' that drained the lives of his mates as they lay screaming for their mothers, had left an indelible scar; branded on his mind forever. Helpless, he'd lain with two useless legs, unable to pull the lads into shade or shelter, barely able to drag his own body into the cover of a half-ruined building. They waited for help, waited for the sound of rescue helicopters; the smell of the dead, overpowering. Faeces, urine and bodily fluids leaked out of men and into the streets. Young boys died on both sides of the field. The sound of a child's screams and a mother's wail as her baby perished in her arms; these were the memories that haunted him. These were the horrors he could never share with anyone. Frank knew that the roses on his bedroom walls were the ghosts of those soldiers, reappearing whenever he closed his eyes, still there when he opened them. He would buy the paint and do it himself if they didn't get on to it in a couple of days. Madge seemed to have understood, perhaps she would get the handyman on the job soon, very soon.

***

Frank missed dinner that evening, he couldn't face the Hyena and couldn't bring himself to be chatty and sociable with the other chaps. He knew he would have to work hard to make friends. He was too damaged. It never occurred to him that others might be too. They were all of a similar age.

His sleep was filled with scenes that had been quiet for years: the scarlet blooms like children's mirror paintings, the scent of tropical flowers like rotten fruit, the purple and orange bougainvillea growing along the walls of the hospital in Townsville, the nurses in starched white uniforms injecting oblivion; masks smelling unaccountably of roses heralding yet another operation and another eon of agony.

He awoke bleary eyed and hungry. He rang reception.

"This is Frank Chambers in No.23. Er ... no, I'm not very well this morning actually. I wonder if I might have some breakfast sent to my room?" He knew his courage to confront a normal social situation was failing him, but he needed more time to collect himself, finish his unpacking and put on his bravest face. "Yes … oh, that's wonderful, thank you. Just toast and coffee would be great. I appreciate it, thanks."

His breakfast arrived but he ate it with little relish. He was still tired after a restless night, but he made the most of the buttered toast with homemade pomelo and mandarin marmalade and plunger coffee. Then he showered, finished his unpacking, closed the wardrobe door, combed what was left of his curly hair, brushed his teeth, then stiffening his spine, left the room.

***

Dulcie woke with a headache. She'd been up a few times in the night, dragged herself to the bathroom in the corner of her room, sitting there for a few minutes willing the business to hurry up so she could go back to bed; her bladder had its own ideas. Consequently, she'd lain awake for hours before dropping off just before her alarm went off.

Her dreams had been punctuated with images of Frank; the real, long-dead Frank. She could see his young face so perfect and beautiful as he went off to war in his soldier's uniform. The train taking him further and further away. His beautiful sculptures punctuated the mishmash of her dreams: swans embracing, bronze figures entwined; he'd been so talented. How she hated those dreams. Whoever this new man was, he was triggering old nightmares, and that alone put her off meeting him. She was beginning to hate this Frank Chambers. How dare he come into her home and do this to her! She'd been happy with the memories of her first love, reasonably happy with the man she'd eventually married, and over the moon with her beautiful daughter, so like Frank to look at she'd almost forgotten his face; she had no photograph of him at all. But the dreams brought him back in stark reality. She already hated the new bloke for simply bringing those dreams back. Not fair after all this time, not fair at all.

Her mobile rang and she jumped.

"Dulcie, where are you? Are you all right, darlin'? Are you coming down, we've got tennis with Lew Hoad today, you know that. You'll be raring to go now that your torture cuff is off." Dottie blathered on while Dulcie squinted at herself in the bathroom mirror.

"I'll be down in a minute Dot. I've only just got up— had a rotten night. Ten minutes."

She showered and dressed, brushed the frizz that had once been her crowning glory, and put some cream on her face, massaging it in upward strokes in the hope they might lift the sag.

She took the lift downstairs, her cane draped over one arm, and shuffled through the lounge into the dining room where Dottie and Dierdre were munching on buttered toast and homemade pomelo and mandarin marmalade.

“Hmm, that’s looks nice,” she said, parking herself beside her friends. She glanced around, noticed the man was not in the dining room, and hooked her cane over the back of the chair.

“What’re you going to do today then, Dulce? Busy schedule, I’ll bet.” Dottie laid her knitting on her lap and scraped the last of the marmalade onto a crust.

“Thought I might pay a visit to Laurie in the Library, get a new book, this one’s a bit of a hard ask.” She delved into her bag and scrabbled around for the book, producing it with a flourish. She couldn’t find the book mark for love nor money but she knew she’d got stuck at the second chapter.

“Well, bother me breathless, I’ve lost the bookmark.”

Dee perked up and pulled a headphone off her right ear. “What’ve you lost, Dulce? Lost your mind again. Bahahaha!”

“Go back to your Chopin, Dee. You’re safer there,” Dottie grinned and put the headphone back on Dee’s ear. “No worries darlin’, Library Laurie will sort you out, you’re a regular customer, aren’t you? I’m sure he won’t charge you fees. Anyway, you can always pay them in kind if he does.” Dottie squawked, then set about clacking her needles again.

“What’re you knitting now, Dot? That’s a different one, isn’t it?” Dulcie fingered the yellow wool.

“Yep, darlin’, this one’s for my new granddaughter, Belle. I told you, didn’t I? Born on the bloody fourth of July. I’ll never hear the end of it now, Daisy’s husbit being a Yank.”

“Oh yes, you did, Dot. I remember now. That’s going to be very pretty, lucky little girl she is.”

"So what made you so late this morning? Bad dreams? Nice dreams?" Dottie chortled.

"No, just my silly old bladder. Up and down like a fiddler's elbow I was, all night long, hardly slept."

"Not this new bloke getting you all in a dither, then?"

"No, no, course not. Nothing to do with whoever he is. I'm going to check out Library Laurie and see if he'll take this one back and lend me another. What do you recommend, Dot? You know your books."

Dottie placed a knitting needle beside her nose. "Something saucy, Dulce? Or something exciting? Bit of both?"

"Bit of both I reckon. Do me good."

"What about *Doctor Zhivago*? Omar Sharif and that pretty Julie Christine. You know we had the movie a couple of years ago."

"Julie Christie, not Christine, Dot. Yes, I remember, made me cry, don't want crying. Something full of suspense, crime maybe."

"I know, I know. Lee Child's *The Affair.* That'll do it. Perfect. Bit of naughtiness, and lots of bad behaviour by nasty people. Just like here really." She chortled again, snorting unattractively into her knitting.

"Right, got it." Dulcie heaved her bones off the chair, grabbed her cane and handbag and bid her friends goodbye. She headed for the back door which led to the doctor's surgery and the Library, happy with her decision. She'd read Lee Child's books before and knew she would be buried in *The Affair* by lunchtime.

Chapter 5

'Love and scandal are the best sweeteners of tea.'
Henry Fielding, Love in Several Masques

The lounge was empty, as was the dining room. Frank looked at his watch and realised that breakfast had long been over. He was now at a loose end, not something he was accustomed to at all. During the last 25 years, he'd been up at dawn, off to the college, back for tea at 6pm and planning his next lessons for the next two hours. Until Beryl had got sick, then everything changed. He wandered towards the veranda and looked out over the maze, his heart tripping a little at the memory of yesterday's panic. The three long chairs where the old ducks had been sitting yesterday were vacant so he took a seat. They were comfortable but he didn't want to get caught there, the chairs seemed to be the province of the three old ducks. He was about to rise and head to the garden again, when his fingers brushed a piece of paper beside the cushion. It was a library ticket for *Anna Karenina.*

He studied it for a moment then put it in his short's pocket.

The uniformed girl he'd seen on his first night at Rosehill appeared at the veranda doors. "Hello sir, can I get you anything? A coffee or a cup of tea?"

"Thank you, that's very kind. Yes, a coffee would be nice. I had a very tasty plunger coffee in my room this morning, would you have some of that?"

"Yes, of course. Would you like a little biscuit to go with it?

"Why not! Hang the expense, give the cat a goldfish!" He chuckled.

"Pardon?"

"I'm sorry, just a silly joke my wife used to tell. Yes, a biscuit would be lovely."

The girl nodded. "Ah, I see. Cat eats goldfish. Yeah, got it. I'll be right back."

The girl disappeared leaving Frank to his thoughts. Why would he tell the poor girl such a stupid joke? It was funny the first time Beryl had said it. He'd laughed at the visual, had even considered a sculpture of a cat pawing a goldfish out of a bowl. Stupid. He peered at the creamy flowers of the handkerchief bushes, considering another walk after coffee. What else does one do in a place like this? I'll have to get to know those other chaps, perhaps they play cards. Maybe a spot of poker. Perhaps there's a games room or something. He hadn't given the mud map that Madge had given him, much more than a passing glance. Maybe there would be some information on it. He could always ask her, of course. He fingered the Library ticket again and peered at it though his new reading glasses. He could go there, maybe they had DVDs as well as books.

The girl reappeared with a tray which she laid on a little table beside the chair.

"What's your name?" Frank said.

"It's Sarah. What's yours?"

"Frank. Just arrived a couple of days ago."

"Yep, I know. Liking it so far, are you?"

"Um, yes. Very nice … nice gardens."

"Yes, they're quite the rage. Don't go in alone though, people have been known to disappear in there and never be seen again. We've lost a good few." She grinned.

"Ha, ha. Yes, so I've heard. You're the second person to mention that. I'd better be careful, make sure I always have my compass with me."

The girl nodded and smiled again. She was a pretty little thing, honey blond hair pulled back in a small pony tail, straggly bits tucked around her ears. Her uniform was pressed and clean and fitted her youthful frame without guile. The uniform was, of course, pink. He'd get used to it, there were worse colours!

"See you again, then," she said, swivelling on low-heeled sandals back to the lounge.

Frank stirred his coffee and nibbled the Tim Tam biscuit that had been laid on the saucer. He must tell Sarah never to put a chocolate biscuit on a saucer beside a hot cup, it melted the chocolate and left the biscuit squishy, even worse if the stirrer was inept and sloshed hot liquid into the saucer. He shuddered.

The day was a little gloomy, some dark clouds hovered over the hills. He imagined he was looking west over the rainforest, the old Gondwanaland forests, so many millions of years old that species of plants and fungi were still being discovered — when ordinary people were able to penetrate the dense undergrowth. He realised his use of 'ordinary people' was totally out of order. Not only did he have enormous respect for the Aboriginal rainforest people, he had experienced rainforest himself in the darkest parts of Vietnam; the darkest, thickest, most dangerous parts of those forests. He knew first-hand how hard they were to penetrate and how the local people knew their hunting pathways like the backs of their hand. He wouldn't want to get lost in there though; it had been bad enough yesterday and he had only been a hundred yards from safety.

He finished his coffee, dabbed the Tim Tam crumbs from his lips and stood, a plan to visit the library and get a really good book firmly embedded in his mind.

***

Dulcie was sitting at a table reading the synopses of a few books. She had put *The Affair* on her right side; it was the favourite so far. After the last of the Lee Child books she'd been studying she decided to have a go at a Grisham. She'd read many of his before but there was a new one out, *Gray Mountain,* and that looked promising too. Laurie had been forgiving when she'd first arrived with a penitent look announcing that she had lost the Library card. He'd given her an admonishing tut, but patted her arm and lead her to the shelves of crime, mystery and suspense books. She had searched the labels and soon found a pile to pour over and thus was completely absorbed when the Library door opened, and the man walked in.

She heard the door bang and looked up. He was standing with his back to her talking to Laurie. She bit her lip, looked at the floor, could she hide under the table? No, ridiculous, stupid, she was going to have to meet him at some time, she knew. But NOT today. She slipped out of her seat and tip toed between the nearest pair of shelves, leaning against the books, her back to the rest of the room, pretending to be studying the labels.

She heard footsteps behind her and held her breath. Don't come in here, please don't come in here. The footsteps continued on and she breathed again. The footsteps had faded to nothing, now she only had to work out how to pick up the books she wanted and hightail it out of the Library.

She turned with great care, her bulk was almost the width of the gap between two shelves, and tiptoed out of the space, checked that the coast was clear, grabbed the two books she wanted to borrow and dashed to the counter. Laurie stamped the two books and gave her two more Library tickets.

"Don't lose these ones please, Mrs Dooley. I don't want to have to order more."

"Thank you, Laurie, I won't. I promise." She made a small pile of the books on the counter.

"May I have these three please, Laurie?" A voice behind said and her heart stopped.

"Yes, of course, Mr Chambers. I'll give you a new card as

you're a new member, and thanks for bringing Mrs Dooley's book mark back."

"No problem, my pleasure."

And before Dulcie could move a muscle, Frank Chambers was right beside her.

"I'm so sorry. I didn't mean to push you out of the way," he said.

"No worries," she muttered, turning her back on him and pulling the books towards her. But her hands were shaking so much she just swiped at them and they fell in a tumble onto the floor.

"Oh, here, let me help you," Frank said and they both bent down awkwardly together.

She lifted her face at the same time as he did and found herself staring into a pair of dark brown eyes over a rather off-centred hook nose.

He bent once more to the books then looked quickly up again. He blinked. His mouth dropped open and he blinked again.

Dulcie shoveled the books into her bag and tried to get to her feet but she'd lost the power in her legs and simply couldn't stand up.

Frank stared at her and she did a quick double take towards him as she struggled off the floor.

"Dulcie?"

She tried to put the bag over her shoulder but even though she was on her feet, she couldn't move.

"Do you two kn…?" Laurie started and both Frank and Dulcie glared at him.

"Dulcie? Really? I thought you were dead."

Dulcie could hardly find her tongue; this could not be happening. "I th … thought you were dead, too."

"You all right, Dulce?" The enquiry from the doorway brought her back to her senses.

"Oh! Dot. Yes. I just dropped all my books and this kind gentleman picked them up for me."

"Oh, you got some, good. Who's this then? Ah, the new chap. Hello. I'm Dorothy, known as Dottie to my friends."

Frank gulped and nodded. "Hello. Yes, I'm Frank, Frank Chambers, just got here yesterday, or was it the day before, I'm not sure now."

Dottie peered at Dulcie and Frank over her specs, backwards and forwards like a tennis match.

"What's going on here? Dulcie?"

"I can't talk about it now, Dot." Dulcie grabbed her bag and fled as fast as she could with her cane over her arm and a bag full of books. She ran into the lift then into her bedroom, slamming the door behind her.

***

Frank! That face, those eyes, that nose, Frank. How could that be?

A thousand families of butterflies had taken flight in Dulcie's tummy. Her heart was stampeding like a herd of stallions. What should she do? The girls could never keep a secret, what was Dottie thinking now? The whole place would be a buzz in no time flat. And Joan? Dear God, what would happen with Joan who had her clutches into him already.

She switched the kettle on. A cup of the Earl would calm her nerves; help her think. She turned to the side table and picked up the silver photograph frame. Long, dark curly hair, just like her father's. Stella's husband Bart and their two children, Daniel, 5 and Becky, 3 — Dulcie's grandchildren — Frank's grandchildren — grinned at her, the happy snapper. Next to Stella was Dulcie's husband, Bob. Dulcie's heart plummeted. Stella, now 48, was due for a visit in a couple of weeks. Dulcie had never told Stella who her birth father was; what was the point if he was dead?

The kettle sang and she remembered the tea bag. The water poured strong and fragrant into her cup. She placed it with the photo frame on the table, and sat again in her big comfy chair. Brought the teacup to her lips. A rap on her door made her start, and she spilled the tea down her front.

“Who is it?” she swiped at the spilled liquid with a tissue.

“It’s us Dulcie, let us in. We have to talk.”

She sighed. She replaced the cup on the table, threw the tissue into the wastebin, smoothed her skirt, and pasted on her most innocent smile. Time to face the music.

“Come in, you two. It’s not locked. What’s the matter?”

“You’re the bloody matter, madam. What’s the matter indeed. Well might we ask you the same thing, young lady?”

Dulcie smiled as Dee hammed up the older sister routine. Dottie had obviously repeated the Library meeting word for word.

Dulcie sighed. “Cup of tea?”

“Thought you’d never ask.” And in a softer tone, “What’s going on, Dulce? You know him, don’t you? Who is he?”

And so, over Earl Grey tea and ginger nut biscuits, Dulcie told her two closest friends in the world, her only two friends in the world, a story she’d never told anyone else. She left nothing out; no point, they might as well know it all.

“You can’t tell a soul, girls. There’ll be hell to pay if anyone finds out. They’d separate us for sure. And I don’t even know if he recognised me!”

“Don’t be so daft, Dulce. He recognised you in a flash, clear as the nose on your face … and his.” Darling Dottie, to the point as always.

The box of tissues was empty; the wastebin full by the time the clock on her bedside table struck six.

“We must have a plan,” said Dee.

“A cunning plan,” snorted Dot.

“We’ll make it work for you, Dulcie; we’ll keep mum.” Dottie and Dierdre were gleaming with delight; it was the most exciting thing to happen in years.

“How do we keep Joan away from him — and let him know that we know?”

“I have an idea, but we’ll have to talk about it tomorrow. Dinner calls and even though I am fed up to the back teeth with wretched ham, salad and tiny, tinned potatoes, I have to eat, fuel my brain even though I’m too tired to plot tonight.” Dulcie smiled at her friends. She knew she was safe.

Chapter 6

'In the country, I always fear that creation
will expire before tea-time.'
Sydney Smith

The next morning the Teapots arrived early at breakfast, determined to get a good start on the day; they had plans to make.

"Hold on girls; I've been thinking." Dulcie held her hands up. "I have to handle the first part of it by myself. I just have to go and talk to him privately, he's bound to be in shock."

Dottie was facing the entrance to the dining room and she stopped mid-chew, the pomelo-and-mandarin-marmalade smothered toast half way to her mouth for the next bite.

Dulcie twisted in her seat and her heart set off on its gallop again as Frank strode into the dining room.

"O … Oh …" said Dierdre.

Dulcie stood up.

"We'll be off then, Dulce … "

"Don't you go anywhere you two," Dulcie muttered under her breath. "We're in this together."

Dulcie gulped and smiled. Frank stopped at their table unsure of what to say.

"Dulcie? Dulcie Thomas? I didn't dare hope…"

"Hello Frank. Yes, it's me. Dulcie Dooley now. And you … I thought you were dead."

"And I thought you were too."

"It's all Australia Post's fault," said Dee, switching her eyes back and forth.

Frank and Dulcie laughed and it broke the ice.

"May I?" he said pointing to the empty fourth chair.

"Of course, please, do sit. Let me introduce you to my dearest friends, Dierdre and Dorothy. Oh, you already met Dottie, yesterday…"

"Yes, in the Library. Hello again, and hello Deirdre."

"Dee, everyone calls me Dee."

They sat and looked at each other in silence for a few moments.

"What…" they began together.

They laughed.

"You go first," Dulcie said.

"No, you. Really. You first, Dulcie. I can't believe I'm saying your name again, after all these years."

Dee and Dottie nodded at each other and rose.

"Best we leave you two to get reacquainted," said Dottie, gathering up her knitting and her *bilum*. Dee collected her headphones and iPod and the pair nodded and grinned and diplomatically departed.

Tears leaked out of Dulcie's eyes and onto the table, but she didn't try to stop them. Frank took a handkerchief from his pocket and mopped the little rivulets from her cheeks. She held his hand to her lips, and tears welled in his eyes. They rolled unbridled down his chin, spit-spotting the table.

They gazed at each other, eyes full. Their foreheads touched and they grinned.

"Frank, listen. We have to be very careful. Let's take a walk."

"I got lost yesterday. It's a jungle out there."

"I know, but I know it inside out. Trust me, I've been lost and found in there more times than — well, you know. But we mustn't be caught. They frown on resident relationships here. They'd have us separated."

“Dr Prince mentioned something about that — said he knew what the old codgers got up to. He must’ve have thought I was an old codger too.” Frank chuckled and rose, pulling Dulcie from her seat.

He let her hands fall and they left the dining room by the veranda doors. They set off across the lawn at a leisurely but appropriately-elderly pace towards the handkerchief bushes where Frank’s adventure had begun the day before. They didn’t see Joan watching them from her high bedroom window. They didn't see the scowl on her face or her fists clenched in fury.

***

Joan turned from the window, her hands balled into fists smacking into her thighs as if she was beating unwanted orange-peeled flesh into submission. She had done that since she was a schoolgirl. She was so tall and heavy, much taller and heavier than all the others in her dorm. She hated being so tall, a head above all the other girls. She had developed round shoulders by the age of 11.

Then one day she met a boy in the Rose Garden behind the quadrangle and he’d been over 6 foot at the age of only 14. She’d really liked him and he her, but boys were forbidden in the Rose Garden, or anywhere else for that matter so she’d started meeting him behind the wall. He had loved the fact that she was tall, he didn’t have to bend down to kiss her, and for the first time in her life she’d felt wanted, felt that tall was good, tall was power, and could be used to her advantage. And she stood up straight and proud again. Laz, short for Lazarus, had been her first lover, there on the leafy forest floor behind the Rose Garden at the age of 13, and he kept coming back for more. Once she’d started her periods they’d had to use Rubber Johnnies, French Letters, which they both hated, but it was better than her getting pregnant.

Once she’d finished school, and finished with Laz, she’d made up her mind that she could have any man she wanted, when she wanted if she stood up tall and proud, and she'd done pretty well until Number Four had died of a heart attack at the age of 78 after a particularly enthusiastic evening.

Joan shoved her hands into her pockets and turned to the mirrored wardrobe doors. The mirrors reflected her orange afro hair, her stylishly clothed body — no need to lower one's standards just because one was living in a retirement home! She was nearly 6 feet tall, 85 kilos — 13 stone in the old money — broad shoulders and hips. She pulled herself out of the slouch she'd recently acquired, tightened long ignored tummy muscles and sucked in her roly-poly belly. She'd need to be at her best if she was to pull Frank Chambers away from that fat, frowsy Dulcie Dooley. What could he possibly see in her?

She strode to the Memory Wall. Four A3 photos were lined up each with a tale to tell beneath them:

Number 1: Todd Holloway, married in 1967, no children, died in 1974, liver cancer. ***** Great lover, soppy date in movies, drank too much but she'd kept his name because he'd been such a good lay.

Number 2: Brett Potts, married 1976, no children, died 1985, colon cancer ****1/2, reasonable lover, teachable but too quick, small penis, drank too much. Kept his name too, quite fun having two hyphenated names. Made her special.

Number 3: Henry Havistock, married 1990, one child — deceased. Divorced 1997, ***1/2, impatient, small penis, drank too much, don't care what happened to him. Didn't bother keeping his name, didn't really want to remember him or the lost child.

Number 4: Martin Jones, married 2001, divine, wealthy, stunning to look at, tall, rode to hounds, aristocratic, brought two brats with him, great in the sack, big penis, drank too much, died of a heart attack 2004. Kept his name too. What's wrong with three hyphenated names? Nothing. I'm special and I can do and have whatever I want.

Number 5: ?

Joan stroked the faces of the three ex-husbands whose names

she'd kept, loving them still in memory. The only child she'd birthed to Henry had died of toxaemia shortly after birth. Joan's affliction at the age of four with Rheumatic Fever had been blamed. Her heart had been a bit dicey ever since, high blood pressure, forever on medication. She never wanted to go through that hell again, but now, yes now, she was ready for Number 5.

She looked around the room. No one had ever been in her suite of rooms on the third floor except her own personal maid, Shirley. It was her private place. It had no roses, no drooping leaves, no patterned anything, not even on the shantung silk, teal-coloured bedspread. The walls were painted a simple off white, a greenish tinge if anything; essence of mint maybe. Little accents in teal highlighted the elegance of the room: her dressing table skirt in sage with teal piping, the padded stool in front of the mirror covered with sage shantung silk, again piped in teal, her curtains, four full-length drops of teal silk piped in sage. The only other colour allowed in her room was the peachy orange throw cushions on her bed which matched her hair. The couch beneath the window was upholstered in the peachy/orange silk and piped in teal; the same window she'd been looking out of when she'd seen Frank — the traitor — walking almost hand in hand with the Dooley bitch.

What was she going to do about that? She'd fallen for Frank already, he was exactly the type of man she wanted for Number 5: tall, handsome, upright, good teeth, nice hands, big hands … Hmmm! Yes, she would have to consider her options carefully. Make a plan. Make him hers.

***

Frank and Dulcie walked with measured paces, matching their steps and sneaking side-long glances at each other as they went. He stroked the creamy petals of a handkerchief bush, letting the sugary dust fall to the ground. Dulcie watched his face and marvelled that he was beside her. She led him through the maze of pathways arriving at a walled garden with a little marble fountain and a pair of bronze dolphins cavorting in the centre. Hedged pink Oleanders enclosed the circular area; two benches faced each other across the dolphins. There was only one way in and one way out so they were safe as long as they watched the entrance.

They held hands and talked; they would need a lifetime to catch up on everything that had happened so they kept their stories to their most recent happenings, planning on working backwards.

Frank told Dulcie about his work with art and sculpture at the college in Townsville; about Beryl and the cancer that had taken her so recently; about Michael.

Dulcie told Frank about Bob, about the cancer that had taken him seven years before; and she cried when she talked of their son Darren who had drowned in the 1974 Brisbane floods. She was about to mention Stella when a shout came from near the entrance to the dolphin garden.

"Dulcie, Frank, where are you? Are you in there?" Dottie rounded the entrance, flushed and panting, her spectacles bouncing on her ample bosom. "They're hunting for you. Joan told them Frank's abducted you. She's set the dogs off. They're coming. Come on, quick, just saunter. Pretend you're — well, you know."

She yelled, "I've found them, they're here! Nothing to worry about, all is well!"

Dulcie and Frank rose and he grabbed her hand. "We'll get together later, don't worry! I'll find a way. Nothing can keep us apart now. I won't let it."

Dulcie grinned and they strolled nonchalantly out of the garden, following the straightest path back to the house. She was suddenly aware of not needing her cane. She'd left it on the chair in the dining room. She was walking like a fifty-year-old.

Halfway back to the house they met Joan, Madge and Dr Prince, all in high dudgeon.

"Goodness me, where's the fire?"

"I saw he'd taken you off, Dulcie. I thought you were in trouble when you didn't come back." Joan was breathing hard, great gasps between words.

"Heavens, no," said Dulcie, "I was just showing Mr Chambers our wonderful garden maze."

Madge took Dulcie's arm and led her towards the house while Dr Prince walked with Frank. Joan marched behind the group eyeing Frank from the rear.

"Warned you," Dr Prince muttered under his breath to Frank.

"Which one should I be most worried about, her behind or her in front?"

"Her behind, and I mean that in every sense of the word, my friend. Be very careful. She's used to getting what she wants." Dr Prince grimaced. Frank wondered if he might have a confidant should ever he need one.

"I'll bear it in mind, thanks." They walked together until the house came into view. Dr Prince shook hands with Frank and took his leave, and Frank carried on towards the dining room. He winked at Dottie and Dierdre who were back in their Laziboys knitting and humming as usual. He was hungry; his breakfast had been metabolized long ago. He'd always been a five-times-a-day man, little and often. He thought it was how he'd been able to keep his figure, nothing stayed in his system for too long. He looked around for Dulcie but she was nowhere to be seen. He wondered if she'd been whisked away for a debriefing. Was he a wolf to be feared? Ridiculous, of course, but he now knew that Joan was going to be a problem.

How much of a problem he couldn't begin to imagine.

Chapter 7

'A woman is like a tea bag,
you never know how strong
she is until she gets in hot water.'
Eleanor Roosevelt

The dining room was empty. Frank looked at his watch and considered his next move. He knew where the Teapots sat — Dulcie had told him that's what they were called because of their figures and their beverage habits— so he took a seat at their table.

Sarah entered from the kitchen swing door and deposited serving dishes full of salads into the servery.

"Hello again, Sarah. Had a good day so far?"

"Nicest part was talking to you Mr Chambers. You're a proper gentleman, not like all of 'em around here, I can tell you."

"Well, thank you. I'll bear that in mind."

The double doors next to the lounge opened and Dottie and Dierdre ambled in heading for their usual table.

"Everything all right, Frank?" Dottie said with a girlish giggle. "That was a funny bit of work earlier wasn't it? You wanna watch out for that Joan. She'll have you for breakfast, lunch and dinner if she can. All with custard and a cherry on top!"

"Dr Prince said I should be careful of her. A bit determined is she once she sets her mind on something?"

"Not half," commented Dee. "She'll be in a right lather if she thinks you like Dulcie better than her. You definitely need a plan, a cunning plan."

"Thanks for the warning. She can't be that bad surely?"

"Ooh. Yes, she can. Mark my words; she can be vicious. She thinks she's the boss round here because she owns half the place and she's been here the longest. But we've been here a fair old time too. We all know how it works. Where the bodies are buried." Dottie cackled, throwing her head back. The cackle turned into a hacking cough and in a second she was red faced and gasping.

Frank lent forward to pat her back, but Dee shook her head. "I've got it. I know what to do here, don't you fret." She rubbed Dottie's back in slow circles, stroking her neck and shoulders. Soon the coughing stopped and Dottie's colour returned to normal.

Dottie laughed again. "Just my old emphysema, Frank. It'll get me in the end. But I'll go out laughing I can tell you."

Before Frank could answer, several residents entered the dining room. The two ladies he'd seen on his first night were in wheelchairs pushed by their partners; they nodded on the way past. The bespectacled Samuel aimed for the servery ignoring Frank completely. Then Joan approached, her hyena grin almost blotting out her face.

"Frank, join me, dear — please?"

He raised his eyebrows at Dottie and Dierdre who glared at Joan as she strode to her table.

"Of course." Frank shrugged, gave a what-could-I-do grimace to the two Teapots and moved to Joan's table taking the seat opposite her.

"I was so disappointed that you chose to do the garden tour with Dulcie Dooley. I was looking forward to showing it to you."

"It just came up in conversation, and off we went. Sorry Joan, I didn't realise you had your heart set on it."

"Huh! I should have known Dooley would get her claws into you. She does it with all the new gentlemen." Joan, passed a finger over the corners of her lips, wiping some of the extra lipstick away.

"That doesn't sound much like her. I found her very obliging."

"Oh yes, obliging indeed. She'll be obliging all the way to your bedroom!"

"Well, I don't…"

"… If you're not too exhausted by that woman already, we'll take a little turn in the garden this afternoon."

Frank hardly knew how to respond, he'd never seen such raw jealousy in his life. "Um … we'll see." Frank got up from the table. "I'm ravenous, going to get some food."

"Would you get me a plate of salad with the cold roast beef? I do like my red meat — please? That would be so kind Frank. Thank you." With no better response available, Frank nodded and headed to the servery.

Dottie and Dierdre were apoplectic. Frank stopped at their table on his way back with two plates of food in his hands. "You'll have a heart attack if you go on like that, Dottie. Dee control her! It might be funny for you, but it's not from where I'm standing. Don't tell Dulcie, she'll die of convulsions."

"Frank, are you coming? The food is getting cold."

"It's already cold, Joan. Not going to get any colder."

Samuel beat him back to Joan's table and for a moment Frank considered giving him Joan's plate and escaping to the Teapots.

Frank placed Joan's food gently on the table. She promptly smothered it with salt and pepper, and without another word piled in as if her life depended on it.

Samuel scowled at Frank and copying Joan, covered his food with salt and pepper as though it were hundreds and thousands on a trifle.

He stared at them astonished, was about to begin on his own plate when he saw Dulcie coming in. He shrugged helplessly as she headed to the Teapots' table. She nodded, and took a seat with her back to him. Dottie and Dee lent forward, and Frank could hear the whispered information being relayed across the condiments.

No sooner had Joan polished her plate than she looked up at

Frank, eyes all wide and innocent. "Oh Frank, would you get me some jelly please. I do like the raspberry one."

"I'll get it for you," said Samuel, hopping up.

"No need, Sam. Sit down. Frank will do it, won't you Frank?"

"Um … of course."

Samuel scowled at Frank again but remained seated.

Frank returned with the jelly. "I'm going to get some coffee, would you like some."

"Oh no, I don't drink coffee; allergic to it for some reason, caffeine not good for my heart. I have such a tender heart." She swooned, her hand on her breast.

Samuel laid his hand on Joan's arm in understanding of her tender heart, but she snatched it away and glared at him.

"Tea would be nice though, Frank. Lots of sugar and a tiny tinkle of milk. Thank you. You are a gentleman."

Frank returned yet again with the coffee and tea, and wondered how he was going to get out of the afternoon's excursion. But he had no hope. Joan grabbed his hand as soon as she'd finished her tea; no matter he hadn't finished his coffee, and marched him out of the dining room.

"Bye bye, Samuel. Frank and I have a garden date!" Joan boomed so everyone could hear.

Frank twisted around to look for Dulcie, but her head was turned away.

Joan launched into a tour commentary once they'd entered the maze. Her talons dug into his flesh as though scared he would run away. She prattled on about various plants and trees. Many of the pathways they took were unfamiliar to him; he hadn't seen them with Dulcie. It was clear that the ten acres of garden were laid out as a maze you could easily get lost in. Frank wondered what the thinking had been behind it. If it had been built as a maze when the house was a family home why wouldn't it have been altered when it became a retirement home?

"This plant here — Frank, are you listening? This plant is, of course, one of the most poisonous plants on the planet. People die from this little beauty all the time." Joan pointed to the pink blooms of the Oleander bush.

"If it's so poisonous, why is it here?"

"Because it's simply beautiful, and even we persons of advanced years don't go around trying to eat it; we just enjoy looking at it. Lovely, isn't it?"

"I suppose so." Frank had no interest in the plants or the conversation. He just wanted the wretched tour to be over. "I'm feeling a little weary, Joan. Do you mind if we go back now?"

"Oh, if we must," she huffed. "I just want to show you this one little place, then we'll go back."

Frank realised with dismay that they'd arrived at the dolphin garden, and he fancied the dolphins were laughing at him as Joan pulled him down to a bench on the opposite side of the one he'd sat on with Dulcie earlier.

"Frank. I must talk to you privately."

"Err … you are Joan. There's no one else here."

"Ah, yes quite. But this is between you and me, no one else, you understand!?"

"Of course. Is there a problem?"

Joan fidgeted, scratched her neck. "You mustn't trust that Dooley woman. She's only out for your money!"

"I don't have any money, Joan. I'm in a retirement home and my son is paying the fees. I don't think Dulcie is like that at all."

"Well, you don't know her like I do. I've seen what she does to new men — any man — when they arrive in the home. She flirts, and simpers and presses them so hard for … um … favours, that she sends them to their early graves! None can handle the pressure."

She sat up straight and patted his knee, proud and happy that she'd been able to save Frank from a fate worse than death.

"But I will take care of you, make sure nothing untoward

happens to you, if you stick with me." She paused. "You do you like me, don't you, Frank?" Joan's thigh was touching his.

He moved his leg. "Um … I hardly know you, Joan. I've only been here a couple of days."

"It's just … I think you're perfect, just wonderful, and I'd hate for you to get tangled up with that Dooley creature. You're just her sort of target, so manly, such a gentleman."

Frank gazed at Joan in astonishment. The Teapots had warned him but he was hard pressed to believe what was happening. He had no idea how to deal with it. If it wasn't so awful it would be funny. But there was nothing funny about her intentions, that was clear.

She took his look of astonishment as tacit agreement and launched into the next part of her plan. She was sure he would never resist her.

"I have missed having a man so much Frank, and you are so much of a man…" She licked her orange lips and moved so close he could smell her lunch.

He lurched to his feet. "I really must get back, Joan. I should be having a nap now — doctor's orders."

"Oh! Are you unwell?" Joan looked aghast, as if her catch was about to drop dead in front of her.

"No, not exactly. I lost my wife recently. I'm still in mourning."

"Oh, you should've told me, I had no idea. I'm willing to wait … until you're fully recovered. You know, I'm a very good catch. I have my own money, I own half of Rosehill, you know and I'm as healthy as an ox. Much better than that Dooley creature! All she knows how to do is read and giggle, and she's sickly. She won't tell you about that, oh no, she'll keep that to herself until she has you in her clutches. Not enough of a woman for you, Frank."

That was it. He rose, bowed and left the dolphin garden.

"Don't get lost, Frank — Frank…"

But he was gone. He counted to twenty to calm his nerves. He could've throttled her.

He was sure he could find his way back to the house; this was after all the same path he'd been on with Dr Prince that morning — more or less.

He found the poinsettias, then the hibiscus, then the handkerchief bushes, and then he was home. Funny, he'd called it home; maybe Dulcie being here had made it home. He strode across the lawn and up the steps to the reception. He didn't see Dulcie coming out of the dining room toilets. He didn't see the dismay on her face as he disappeared up the stairs.

Dulcie rejoined the Teapots in their Laziboys. Dee was humming along with one of her Strauss waltzes and Dottie was knitting furiously, the baby's yellow cardigan all but finished.

"Wanna get this little number finished before the weekend, Dulce. My Trisha's coming up. Can't wait to see little Belle — cute as a button she is."

"I'm going to go up for a nap girls. It's been a bit of a day. See you at dinner."

"Ok, then darlin.' Have a good one." Dottie waved a knitting needle at Dulcie, and nudged Dee who performed a conductor's three-time swish with her hand.

***

Frank delayed his arrival at dinner until he could be sure the Teapots would be seated. He felt like a wimp but he didn't want to be pounced upon again. He peeked around the door into the room, and saw that all the usuals were seated. Dulcie gave him a sweet smile as he approached and his heart lurched.

Joan waved her arm at him.

He strode to the Teapots' table pretending he hadn't seen Joan's invitation, and took the seat between Dulcie and Dottie. Dee was plugged in. Dottie nudged her, and when she saw that Frank had arrived she took the headphones away from her ears. Swan Lake blasted the congregation; some residents smiled whilst others grimaced.

“They’ve got no taste most of these ignorant beggars,” said Dierdre. “I don’t mind if they like it or not — I do. Do you like the classics, Frank?”

“I do, very much Dee. As an artist, music of all sorts fits into my world.”

“What sort of artist are you then?” Dottie laid her knitting on her lap.

“A sculptor mostly, but I taught art for forty odd years in Townsville, so I don’t have a very large collection of my own work. I’d love to get back to it though. Dulcie was very good; a wonderful painter, weren’t you, Dulcie?”

“Frank … oh Frank!” Joan’s voice scythed through their conversation. “Aren’t you coming to sit with me?”

Frank glanced at Dulcie then down at his food. “Not tonight, Joan, thank you. I’ll chat to these ladies tonight. Bon Appetit.”

Joan harrumphed behind them and Samuel whinnied, “It’s alright Joanie, you’ve got us — me and Prudence, you don’t need him!”

“You’ve got no conversation, Sam. Frank’s intelligent, a man of the world, a real conversationalist.”

“Why do you bother sitting with us then if you don’t like us — why bother?”

The Teapots felt sorry for Sam, but he put his head on that block every day.

Dulcie returned to their topic. “I wasn’t bad, I suppose. Most of my painting was done to help Bob with his architectural drawings — you know elevations and artist’s impressions. It didn’t really tax my imagination, and I’d still love to do that. Probably, too late though.”

“It’s never too late darlin’— for anything. Is it Frank?” chuckled Dee.

“No, Dee, it isn’t.” Frank grinned. He liked these Teapots.

Behind them, Joan seethed, Samuel consoled, and Prudence worried her food around her plate.

***

The following morning Frank and the Teapots were seated early for breakfast. They'd received a note under their doors the night before. It announced an excursion the following day. The notice was confusing but clarification had been promised. The Superintendent of the home, Major Paul Longley, whom people hardly ever saw, would address them the following morning and all would be made clear.

The notice said: 'All persons of an ambulant capacity are invited for an excursion to Trinity Beach for a day of fun and/or frolic. Bar-B-Q will be provided.'

Frank and Dulcie looked around the room. Joan was not there. Samuel and Prudence were in their usual seats. Sam scanned the minuscule crowd for the carrot-headed amazon.

"It's your fault," he hissed, as Frank carried two plates of bacon and eggs to their table.

"What's my fault, Sam?"

"Just being here is your fault. It's pushed her all off kilter. She's a delicate flower."

Frank deposited the plates on the table and raised an eyebrow. "Delicate flower?"

Dulcie said, "Sam's been besotted with Joan for years. And she doesn't know he even exists, poor soul."

"Ah, that explains his dislike of me then. Why doesn't he tell her?"

"Sam doesn't think he's good enough for her. Every time a new man arrives, she mounts a campaign to nab him. In her life before Rosehill, she had four husbands, one at a time obviously." She chuckled. "Three of them died, and one divorced her but she was left rich. Now all she wants is another one. Fifth time lucky she reckons, so she launches herself at the new chaps the minute they arrive, just like she's done with you, hoping to get you before you have a chance to realise what's hit you." Dulcie took a bite of her toast. "Unfortunately, the last one, Terry Maidens, was so terrified of her he upped and had a heart attack when she was in his room attempting some — you know. That's why they made the 'no visiting other residents' rooms' policy. Joan's a loose cannon."

Frank thought back to Joan's accusations of Dulcie for exactly the same thing. He knew people often accused others of what they are doing themselves but he wondered if her jibe about Dulcie being sickly might have a foundation in reality. He made a note to himself to ask her later.

Just then a small kafuffle drew their attention. Paul Longley, a short, portly man with a shiny pate and bushy red sideburns, marched into the dining room accompanied by Madge and another lady Frank remembered from the doctor's surgery. Any hair Longley had ever sported on the top of his head had migrated to his bushy cheeks, and it was clear from their lustre that he cared for them with diligence.

"Your attention campers, please." Longley, a retired major from the British army chuckled at his little joke. "Here to tell you about tomorrow's excursion. So exciting, won't it be, Pamela?" He grabbed one of her hands and hoisted it above her head. "This is Dr Prince's nurse and receptionist, in case you healthy people haven't been to see him recently. Only been here a few weeks, haven't you, my dear? Pamela will be your escort tomorrow together with Dr Prince, and Madge whom you all know, of course. I won't be going, but golly, you're going to have a rip-roaring time at Trinity Beach. Now hands up who's steady enough on their pins to take a walk on the promenade — except it's an esplanade. Ha! Ha!"

Frank and the Teapots looked at each other, nodded then tentatively raised their hands. Sam and Prudence poked their heads up and nodded, the two partnered-pairs shook their heads — wheelchairs would be awkward — but another single gentleman, Mike Partridge, put his hand up.

"Joan'll come too," said Samuel.

"That makes eight then. Jolly good. A perfect busload. On parade at 09.30 then. Front steps! Excellent! Don't forget your togs, hats, and sun cream. You know the drill — excellent!" and off he strutted.

But Joan didn't appear at breakfast that morning, or at all during the day. A minor concern flitted through the lounge like a dying butterfly while people slept or read, played cards or mahjong, while Dulcie and Frank wandered the gardens, while Dottie knitted and Dierdre hummed. She didn't arrive for dinner either; by this time Samuel was beside himself.

"Has anyone been up to Joan's room, Madge?" said Sam at the reception desk. "It's not like her to miss meals you know."

"Now, Sam, you know that we can't just go barging into someone's room just because they've missed a meal or two. But, between you and me, she did have breakfast in her room this morning. I'm sure she's fine; stop your worrying, dear." Madge knew about Samuel's unrequited love for Joan. Everyone did — except Joan. He harrumphed away knowing he'd get into trouble if he went upstairs to investigate.

Chapter 8

'Come along inside. We'll see if tea and buns can make the world a better place.'

The Wind in the Willows

Perfect autumn weather in North Queensland brings wagonloads out to the beaches.

The trip to Trinity Beach thirty kilometres down the winding mountain road afforded the elderly residents and their chaperones an alternative landscape to the tropical gardens of Rosehill. Hibiscus and Poinsettia gave way to Coconut Palm and Indian Almond, Terminalia and brightly coloured Ixora.

Dr Prince, the designated driver for the day, parked beside the Watersports van on Trinity Beach's Vasey Esplanade. The kilometre-long beach was already dotted with sun worshippers: children jumping on bouncing castles tethered to the sea bed, paddle-boarders battling to keep their balance in the swell beyond the beer-froth waves, and two-man kayaks slicing through the ocean with the deliberate rhythm of the enthusiastic amateur.

The Hiace disgorged its geriatric load on the tarmac. Samuel was miserable. Joan had not appeared that morning. Prudence hung on his arm, her gamy left leg affording an excuse to be physical. His blindness to her adoration matched Joan's blindness to his.

Mike Partridge, Frank and the Teapots were delighted to have a Joan-free day. Mike, a ruddy-coloured, skittle-shaped man in his late seventies was the owner of flowing white locks that reminded everyone of Doc in the *Back to the Future* films. He had also been a target of Joan's seductive ploys several years earlier when he'd first arrived at the home, and he'd heard about Frank's dilemma through the efficient Rosehill grapevine. He settled himself into the seat next to Frank, planning to verify the rumours, and find out more about the latest 'mark'.

Frank and Dulcie had discussed seating arrangements before leaving, and agreed not to be seen in each other's company too much for fear of setting tongues wagging. With an imperceptible shrug acknowledging this eventuality, Dulcie parked her beach bag on the seat behind Dr Prince. When Pamela Evans gave her a please-may-I look Dulcie moved the bag immediately, and the two ladies were soon deep in conversation about the books of Somerset Maugham and Agatha Christie, Baldacci and Child, but not *The Affair* which Dulcie had borrowed but had yet to open.

Dottie and Dee took a brace of seats behind Dulcie and Pamela; Dee, her whiskered chin snuggled into her chest, was happily engrossed in a Debussy nocturne and Dottie was daydreaming out the window. Dottie had brought her knitting in a plastic bag wrapped in a towel that she'd crammed into her *bilum* along with the kitchen sink. The capacious, multicoloured string bag was a souvenir of her time spent in Papua New Guinea as the wife of a structural engineer. Ten years of her life had passed in that country where things were easy, the babies were taken care of by the *hausboi,* and her husband was still the man of her dreams. The bag had outlasted the marriage by fifteen years; no fault of hers that her husband had fallen for a doe-eyed beauty, and chosen the road to divorce and financial ruin.

Both girls had brought their bathing costumes and were determined to indulge in a salt-water dip. Dulcie refused to even consider bringing hers; no way was she going to show her body to Frank until she felt more secure. She had some big news for him this day, and had no idea how he would take it; it could be the end of everything.

***

Joan giggled to herself and rubbed her hands in glee as she watched Frank and the Teapots board the bus. She spied Samuel, anxiety creasing his forehead, searching for her as usual, and she guffawed as Prudence grabbed his arm.

Once the bus was out of sight, Joan left her room and went downstairs to the reception. Sandra, Madge's second in command, was in place behind the desk and she smiled as Joan approached.

"How can I help you today, Mrs Holloway-Potts-Jones?"

"I'd like a taxi please, Sandra; order one for me, there's a good girl." Joan walked into the lounge and sat in one of the Teapots' Laziboys.

She bounced up and down and stroked the pink, velveteen upholstery making it squeak. "Hmm. You'll keep," she murmured.

"Taxi'll be here in ten minutes, Mrs Holloway-Potts-Jones. Do you need anything to take with you?"

"Not today ... thank you." Joan always spoke curtly to the staff, she had no illusions that they were of the same class as her, but she tried, at least, to be polite. It never occurred to her that she could allow them to call her Ms Joan, or even just Joan. Standards must be observed. Even when you had a triple-barrelled name.

The taxi dropped her off on Grafton Street in the Cairns CBD with a promise to pick her up in a couple of hours.

The first shop would only take a short while since she had her list well prepared. The second would take a bit longer.

It was time for lunch when Joan emerged from shop number two, and nearly two o'clock before she was back in her room at Rosehill. Once her parcels were stowed, she took the stairs down to Dulcie's bedroom. The laundry and cleaning cart was outside the room next to Dulcie's; a blue room belonging to Mike Partridge; a more boring man you couldn't hope to meet in Joan's opinion, but that was neither here nor there at that moment since he was off on the bus with the others. She'd had her fun with him when he first arrived but he'd proven to be dull, uninspiring, sexually lacking; a total waste of space. She'd moved on with alacrity to the next victim, Terry. But that had ended in disaster. Were there no red-bloodied men in their seventies left? She had high hopes for Frank if she could get him away from the Dooley cow. Joan slipped into Dulcie's room undetected.

She removed her shoes, aware that the wooden floors beneath the carpets might give her presence away, and padded into the bathroom to carry out the first part of her plan. Once completed, Joan explored the bedroom, peering at an empty silver photo frame. She waggled her head back and forth in disapproval of Dulcie's choice of books on the bedside table until, noticing a key lying on the top of *The Affair,* she grinned to herself and slipped it into her pocket.

Happy with her afternoon's work, she checked herself in the mirror, smiled joyfully at her reflection, replaced her shoes and left the room locking the door behind her.

***

After the Bar-B-Q lunch of greasy sausages, steaks and bread, with a handful of wilted rocket leaves thrown in, Dottie and Dee parked themselves on a timber-slatted bench just off the footpath; Dottie attending to her kntting, and Dierdre off with Mr Mozart. The wind had risen to more than a gentle sea breeze, so they'd gone off the idea of a swim. Frank and Dulcie had wandered towards the southern end of the beach. A bench with a view was Dulcie's objective; a seat set on the rocks overlooking Yorkey's Knob Marina to the south and Double Island to the north. Aware that their lives were still full of restrictions, they had avoided holding hands on the path.

They arrived at the bench after much more of a climb than Dulcie had bargained for, and Frank took a towel from his bag and laid it on the seat. Dulcie sat facing him, the wind whipping her shoulder length curls into standing corkscrews. She scrabbled in her beach bag and pulled out an envelope that she placed on her lap.

"Frank, there's something I haven't told you yet and it's something very important. Something you really need to know."

Intrigued, Frank grinned the impish grin that had won her heart so many decades ago, but shut his mouth with a clunk when he realised she was serious. "What could that possibly be?"

"This, Frank. This." Dulcie drew a photograph from the envelope. The brisk south-easterly wind had other ideas, grabbing the edge of the photo and ripping it out of Dulcie's hand. "No! No!" she yelled, lurching to her feet.

Frank didn't know whether to hold on to her or chase after the photo that was already halfway down the rocky embankment on its way to a watery grave.

"No! Oh, no!" Dulcie cried again, covering her face with her hands.

"What was it Dulcie? What was it — a photo?"

"I can't tell you now — the wind has spoilt it! I can't, not now. You wouldn't understand. Oh, dear!"

"Of course, I'll understand. You can tell me anything. You know you can."

But Dulcie was inconsolable. She would have to find another way. It would have to wait. It wouldn't be long now anyway.

"No, Frank. Another time. We'd better be getting back — don't you think? It'll take me forever down those steps and I didn't bring my cane."

Frank shook his head, perplexed. He had barely seen the offending photo — just a few people.

Mindful now of the gale bullying their light jackets, they rose cautiously and hung on to each other as they negotiated the rocky slope between the seat and the steps. Dulcie's legs were aching by the time they reached the Esplanade; she should have brought her stick. She clung onto Frank's arm until they reached the bus.

Dottie and Dierdre peered at them when they rounded the corner, and Dottie raised her eyebrows in expectation. Dulcie shook her head.

Dr Prince, his round face pink from the sun and wind, accompanied Pamela up the sandy slope from the beach. They were walking very close together; for support perhaps the Teapots thought. Hah!

"Time to be heading back to the hills boys and girls. I'll get everyone rounded up. If you four would like to hop in— you know what I mean— get on the bus and get settled, that'd be great. We'll be leaving in about ten minutes— I hope." Dr Prince trotted off in search of the others.

Pamela opened the Hiace door and Frank and the Teapots clambered in, taking the same seats they'd had before.

Dulcie was sulking; she couldn't help it. She'd been gearing herself up for the big announcement and now it would have to wait.

Pamela Evans was also quiet on the way back. She had a wet towel wrapped around her body, sarong style, and having not taken advantage of the beachside shower, her long, grey-blond hair was still salty from the ocean. Mike followed her like a bedraggled puppy, his white hair wilder than usual as he puffed his way up the grassy slope to the vehicle.

The journey back to Rosehill was uneventful. Frank chatted to Mike, but kept replaying the lost photo incident in his mind; it baffled him still. Mike became quiet once he realised Frank wasn't listening, and they finished the last few kilometres in silence until they reached the top of the hill. Rosehill — home.

Chapter 9

*'Find yourself a cup; the teapot is behind you.
Now tell me hundreds of things.'*
Saki

An atmosphere of anticlimax hung in the air as the residents exited the bus, placing their sandaled feet on the gravel and peering up at the old house as if they'd never seen it before. The Teapots went through the Reception to the lift.

"Debrief?" said Dottie.

"Hmm. Think we should," nodded Dee.

"Mine?" said Dulcie.

"Good idea — put the kettle on."

On the landing outside Dulcie's bedroom door, she reached for the handle to let them all in. But it was locked. The three looked at each other and shrugged; this was not uncommon. They so rarely left the home that they never needed to lock their doors. The cleaning staff didn't usually bother either; must be a new person on the crew.

Dulcie scratched in her bag like a chicken pecking for scraps hunting for her key. "That's odd. I usually take it with me, just in case, but I can't find it — sure I had it — I think. I'll go down to the desk and borrow theirs, won't be long." Dulcie was back within minutes with the spare. "Don't let me forget to give this back to Madge before dinner, girls."

Dulcie's kettle hummed its readiness while the others organised cups and saucers, milk, sugar and biscuits and parked themselves wherever they could.

"So, what happened?" Dottie said.

Dulcie reached into her bag and retrieved the empty envelope. Two cups of tea and a whole packet of custard creams later, they'd heard it all. And had no solutions.

"Can I borrow your la-ta, Dulce?" said Dee, rising from her chair.

"You don't need to borrow it dear, you can have it for the duration." They all chuckled.

A piercing shriek interrupted them. "God, what've I done? There's wee all over the floor!" Dulcie and Dottie heaved themselves up and made for the bathroom. There were yellow puddles decorating the white tiled floor!

"Did you miss, darlin'?" Dottie grinned; they'd all been there.

"No, I didn't bloody miss, look!"

"Do we have to?"

"Yes, you do. Look!"

They tiptoed between the puddles and there, stretched tight over the top of the lavatory pan was a thin film; a shiny skin; a stretched piece of Glad Wrap — Dee's pee had hit the transparent film and dribbled over the edge and on to the floor; the only warning was the lack of tinkling noises into the pan. Dee hadn't realised until it was too late.

They looked at each other.

"Pull your knickers up, Dierdre. Make yourself decent and let's have a think." Dottie took charge.

"You think while I clean this up," said Dulcie.

"No, dear God, no! I'll do that. You two think!" Dee reached for a towel from the handrail and laid it on the floor. "Going to need a few of these I think," she mumbled. "Got any more towels, Dulce?"

"No, but I've got some you-know-what pads. They soak up wee, let's use those!"

“Didn’t know you used those,” said Dottie.

“Don’t … um … really, but I have them just in case I forget my pelvic floor exercises and get a little out of trim, you know,” said Dulcie, on all fours laying white pads over the urine. “Heaven’s above Dee, how big a bladder have you got, there’s enough here to sink a battleship.”

“Looks like a yellow and white chequered bedspread.”

“You wouldn’t want that on your bed darlin’!” Dottie chuckled. “Let’s let that soak for a while girls, we need to ponder.”

It didn’t take long.

“Joan!”

“Where’s my key?” said Dulcie rising from her armchair. “Where is it? I left it here on my book — I think. It’s not here!”

“Joan!”

“Why would she take my key? What good can that do her?”

“She’s got access to your room any time she likes if she has your key; she can do whatever she wants in here.”

“But why would she want to? Am I being really stupid, girls? Why would she want to do this; and that — in the la-ta, why?”

“Aye, and there’s the rub darlin.’ She wants your Frank. She wants her Number five, and it looks like she would do anything to get him.”

“Well, she can’t bloody well have him. She wants a fight, she’ll get one. I can’t believe she would anything so childish, this is pathetic. I feel sorry for her. Whatever will she do next?”

“Let’s get ourselves cleaned up for dinner, girls. Dulce, you can come to my place, have a shower there.”

Dulcie nodded and grabbed her toiletries then padded bare foot three doors down, to Dottie’s room. The stinky, wet, yellow pads on her bathroom floor made having a shower in there out of the question.

Once refreshed the Teapots took the lift downstairs, returned the key to Madge, told her about the ‘accident’ and headed to the dining room. Madge promised the mess would be taken care of before bedtime.

They hadn't decided how to handle Joan; whether to confront her or leave it alone for the time being; after all, they had no proof. The dining room was empty apart from Sarah setting the tables.

Dulcie wondered where Frank was, whether he'd guessed what it was that she'd tried to show him … tell him.

The dining room filled slowly. Samuel appeared, sunburn on his fluffy white head. Prudence limped to the table and Samuel pulled the chair out for her; she smiled.

No Joan.

The partnered pairs rolled in and took their usual seats, nodding a greeting.

Still no Joan.

***

If it had been one minute earlier or later, it never would have happened. But it wasn't and it did and she saw it as a sign.

Frank entered the lift when it stopped at the second floor. If he hadn't taken a step to get into the lift he would have turned tail for Joan was already there and the last thing he wanted was another confrontation with her. But he was too late, he couldn't pull his leg back, he'd have over balanced and that would have been worse, so he carried on into the lift. Frank managed a small smile. " Good evening, Joan."

Joan took his words as approval of her new look and grabbed his hand. She pulled him closer to her, thrusting her chest towards him, and pushing his face into her cleavage. He was suffocating in red nylon. "We're going to be so good together, you and me, Frank. You'll see. We're perfectly matched."

Frank struggled free. "No, no, this cannot be, Joan. You don't understand." His sense of courtesy took hold and he wimped out. "You're much older than me, Joan. It wouldn't work."

"Oh, I love a toy boy, Frank. Your youth matches my experience."

"I'm no toy boy. I'm 73!"

"And I am the most vigorous 77 year old you'll ever know. Be proud, don't be afraid. I'll look after you like no other woman ever could. Come here, Frank."

Frank backed into the corner of the lift as it made its leisurely way to the ground floor. But there was no escape, she was all over him like a spider web. He wanted to push her away, but feared he would hurt her and she would call foul. On top of the horrendous new bleached-blond beehive hair-do she stunk of cheap perfume.

She dragged him by the hand into the dining room, her hyena grin so firmly planted it looked as if she'd had botox to keep her lips lifted at the sides like the Joker in the Batman films. Frank tried to pull his arm away but she had him in her claws, her cherry red nails digging into the soft flesh of his inner arm. Joan was delirious; her laugh, deranged. He cringed as she pulled him past the Teapots' table and pushed him on to his designated seat.

Dulcie's face was a mask of horror, her expression searing his brain. Frank wanted the floor to open up beneath him. He tugged his arm away but Joan dug her claws in harder. He prayed that Dulcie would understand; he would never be able to justify his cowardice.

A hush fell on the assembled few and all heads craned towards her and the unfortunate man by her side. Joan Holloway-Potts-Jones posed as if awaiting photographers, her talons digging into his sleeve and holding Frank captive. A red Lycra sheath enclosed her Amazonian figure emphasising every bulge. Six inch, red, patent-leather shoes along with the extra high hair-do made her loom monstrously over her captive. Like an octopus, she'd imprisoned him; her red lips smirking, teeth made yellow by the scarlet lipstick.

She sashayed like a queen, around her table as if she were doing some sort of cabaret act, then stopped beside Sam and peered down her nose at his horror-struck face.

"Samuel. Take Prudence to another table. Frank and I want some privacy." He hurried to his feet, pulling Prudence with him.

Joan glanced sideways at Dulcie and sneered.

Dee whispered across the table to her best friend. “Are you sure you want this man, Dulce? Not standing up for himself is he — being a bit of wimp, I’d say.”

Dulcie bent her head for a brief moment then sat up straight. “I am not going to be cowed by that woman. She thinks she can steal my man, she’s got another think coming. The Army might’ve taken him from me once, but Joan Holloway-stupid-Potts-Jones will not have him this time.” Dulcie rose from the table, her head held high. She strode to the servery to help herself to a large portion of cottage pie and peas, and returned to her table without a backward glance.

“This is war, girls! This is war!”

Chapter 10

'The very act of preparing and serving tea encourages conversation... Even the tea itself – warm and comforting, inspires a feeling of relaxation and trust that fosters shared confidences'
Emilie Barnes, If Teacups Could Talk

Joan's joyful ownership of Frank Chambers at dinner instigated self-congratulatory eye rolling every time she caught someone's glance. Her victory was evident for all to see. Most avoided her and Frank picked at his food hoping to get dinner over and escape as fast as he could.

The Teapots left the dining room shortly after Joan and Frank's arrival, eating quickly and taking bowls of rice pudding to Dottie's room.

"Has she finished, do you think?" said Dulcie. "Has she done her worst and got her prize?"

"Oh, Dulce! You know he doesn't want to be there. That's obvious. Poor bugger, he's been nabbed each time and he's too polite to refuse. 'Bout time he did though."

Dottie finished pouring the last of the Merlot into three small glasses, a forbidden tipple she kept very quiet about. She knew the cleaners either never cleaned under her bed or simply knew the stash was there and said nothing; maybe they even helped themselves to a little nip every now and then; the bottles sometimes seemed emptier than they should. The Teapots toasted each other, but they were quiet;

the toxic atmosphere in the dining room had affected them all.

A knock at the door alarmed them. Dottie padded to the door in her bare feet.

"Who is it?"

"It's Frank. Is Dulcie there? She wasn't in her room."

Dottie raised her eyebrows at Dulcie, who nodded quickly, and Dottie unlocked the door to let Frank in. "Yes. Come in. But you must be quiet."

Frank entered the room and immediately went to Dulcie's side. "I'm so sorry, my darling. She grabbed me in the lift — she's got my whole life planned out. No. 5 Husband. I have to get away from her, but I don't know how. I just made an excuse that I needed to go to the bathroom, and bolted. She's a nightmare!"

"Oh, Frank! You have no idea. You won't believe what she was up to while we were at the beach!"

Frank's heart sank while Dulcie described what had happened; the disappearance of her key and the indignity of the cling film prank.

But when she'd finished her tale, the four of them collapsed into giggles. It had been too funny for words, poor Dee with her knickers round her ankles knee deep in piddle. Eventually, with another glass of Merlot in hand they settled down realising they needed to take the whole escapade seriously.

"She's dangerous, Frank. She's unpredictable," said Dottie. "She has her heart set on you and kidnap is not beyond her. She thinks you'll be hers. I think somewhere she really believes she can still have a child, one that survives. She's mad! But not so mad that it's obvious."

"We have to fight fire with fire!" Dee was headphone free for a change.

"The time for pussy footing around is over. We either have to report her, or fight back. We are the Teapot Gang after all!"

"The Teapot Gang? I thought it was just the Teapots," Frank hooted.

"Yes, that's we call ourselves," said Dulcie. "Silly I know, but we like it, makes us believe that life's little adventures are not yet over!"

"No, it's great, I like it. Dr Prince told me I should watch out for her, but she keeps catching me when I least expect it. What can we do? Do you think she'll be satisfied after this evening's parade?"

"Unlikely, she thinks she's had a win. Unless of course she takes the fact that you bolted, personally," said Dottie. "But if you vanish into thin air she's going to arc up and blame Dulcie. Somehow we have to hide you, or neutralise her. Anyone got any thoughts?"

"I have an idea, but it's cutting a very short course across a very long ocean." Frank clasped his hands between his knees and looked into the eyes of each Teapot.

"And?" Dierdre and Dottie leaned forward in their chairs.

"What if we announced that Dulcie and I are to be married?"

Dottie spoke first. "Might be worth asking Dulcie first, don't you think?"

Dee piped up, "It's going to look odd. You and Dulcie appear to have only just met."

"Yes, but even if the explanations have to come later, it might put Joan off the scent," said Frank.

"So, are you suggesting that you would only say that you and Dulcie were getting married, but not actually mean it?" said Dottie.

"Oh God, no, of course not. I've always wanted to marry Dulcie; we were engaged before I was called up to fight for my country. I'd marry her in an instant — if she'll have me."

Dulcie had been silent during this exchange, watching the protagonists as they rearranged her life. Dottie and Dee looked at Dulcie. Dulcie looked at Frank.

Frank put his hand out, reaching for Dulcie's. He moved to the floor beside her chair, his knees creaking loudly, and looked up at her.

He smiled; that magical smile not changed by age, nor diminished by the scars of war.

"Will you, Dulcie? If it's not too late, will you Dulcie Thomson be my wife?"

"I'm Dulcie Dooley now, Frank. Needs to be right, don't you think?"

"Oh, of course, I forgot. So, now. Dulcie Dooley, would you please, only fifty years late, do me the honour of becoming my wife?"

"We ought to leave the room, Dot, don't you think?" Dee said.

"You stay put you two." Dulcie laughed. "Of course, I'll marry you and be your wife till the end of never, till the end of forever. The same as I said fifty years ago, Frank Chambers; nothing has changed for me, only the picture in the mirror."

"Now we should definitely leave the room, Dot," said Dee getting up.

"But it's my room. If there's going to be shenanigans, they can go to their own room." Dottie grinned as Dulcie and Frank embraced, chaste and sweet.

"I love you," Frank whispered in Dulcie's ear.

"I love you, too," said Dulcie much louder than she intended.

Dottie and Dierdre clapped their hands and laughed. They all laughed. Then Dottie put her fingers to her lips. "Ssh! You lot. We'll be busted. This has to remain between us only — until we're ready. Go to your own beds now and we'll make a plan tomorrow. Pencils and notebooks at the ready for breakfast! Go, you two. Congratulations! We'll have to be renamed now. The Four Teapots."

Frank walked Dulcie to her room, and pausing at the door, they faced each other.

"Do you mean it, Frank? It's not just a ploy to get rid of Joan?"

"Oh God, Dulcie, of course I mean it. I've never stopped loving you. You've always been here in my heart, wherever I've been and whatever I've been doing."

"I daren't ask you into my room, we'd by hung out to dry if they found out — and anyway it might not be smelling the best." Dulcie chuckled and rested her head on his chest.

"My darling, if I came in, I'd never leave. No, we'll have to wait." He kissed her grey corkscrew ringlets.

She looked up at him. "You're right of course, we've waited this long, we can wait a bit longer. There is something important I need to tell you though. Perhaps tomorrow we can find some private time."

Frank bent his head and lightly touched her lips with his. She'd never forgotten his ability to light a fire in her with his butterfly touch; she felt the adrenalin thump in her nether regions.

"I'd better go in. You're making me all unnecessary."

They kissed again, and Frank squeezed her hand. "Until tomorrow, my love."

Dulcie was exhausted, too much for one day. She couldn't stop thinking about what Joan had done, assuming it was her, of course. She chuckled at the memory, it was such a ridiculous scene, but also a pathetic prank by a grown woman.

As she pulled her nightie over her curls, she wondered if she would sleep. Her head was full of Frank, the wonder and the terror about what Joan would do next. She tumbled into bed, laid her specs on the side table and was asleep within a second.

***

The Teapots, all four, made it to breakfast early, serving themselves with bacon and eggs, toast and pomelo and mandarin marmalade, tea and orange juice. They were starving hungry as if they hadn't eaten the night before. Perhaps with all the drama of the blond bombshell in the red lamé dress, their appetites had not been so rabid.

Eating irons to one side, out came the notebooks. Dottie was voted scribe and a clean page was found.

"How do we fight this? Do we simply ignore it, pretend it didn't happen? Do we tell the Major? Do we throw the book at Joan? She could deny it, of course, she would. How do we trap her into admitting what she did?" Dottie wrote all the questions down in her book then looked at the other three for comment.

"You're right Dot, we have no proof. She left no fingerprints. We could announce it all to the other residents, say how hilarious it was because Dee had tried to throw a tissue down the loo, and it had just sat there. And that's when we noticed the cling film, and thought the maid had left it by mistake." Dulcie had had a good night's sleep and was full of ideas.

"Actually, that's a great idea, darling," said Frank.

"Yes. It would infuriate Joan, because she would think she'd failed. Then maybe she'll try something else, but this time we'll be ready for her." Dee nodded enthusiastically, she'd even arrived at breakfast without her iPod and headphones attached. They were in her bag for later though.

A sense of purpose ran through the group. A sense of teamwork; all for one and one for all.

They looked around the dining room, but there was no Joan. They could hardly play the scene without her present. In fact, looking around, they were the only ones in the dining room. No one else had come down.

Dottie said, "Perhaps they've all taken breakfast in bed because they know that the vision of Joan in her red lamé dress has put them off their food for life."

"It didn't put me off my food." Dee giggled. "Mind you it takes a lot to put me off my food, as you well know, girls."

"I'll go and have a word with Madge, and see if everyone took their brekkie in their rooms. We'll have a lovely peaceful day if they did." Dottie got to her feet and waddled to the reception.

"Perhaps you and I can take another turn in the garden, Dulcie. You had something you wanted to tell me." Frank touched Dulcie's hand and she curled her palm into his.

"Yes. A good idea. Let's do that."

Dottie's loud voice greeted their ears. "Good morning, Joan, how spectacular you looked last night. Quite the star."

They glanced towards the reception from where Dottie had made her announcement. They could see Joan with a little group around her making a casual but deliberate entrance.

"I'd better go, Dulcie, you stay. I can't be near the woman." Frank hopped to his feet and escaped via the exit towards the Doctor's surgery and the Library. He was gone before Dulcie could say anything, or Joan could see him.

Joan sashayed into the dining room followed by Sam and Prudence, limping gamely behind. After them came the two partnered pairs, wheelchairs and all. It was as if Joan had summoned a posse.

At least her garb was less alarming, only a pair of studded Levis, a cowboy shirt and hat. She drew two tables together instructing the Stillwells and the Smithsons to park themselves at the far end while she held the centre spot flanked by Sam and Prudence.

Dulcie realised there was no way they could put on the performance they had planned; Joan had stacked the deck. So she and Dee collected their plates and cutlery and took them to the servery.

"Leaving so soon, Mrs Dooley?" Joan cawed. "Where's your other little playmate today? Hiding from you … or from me?"

Dulcie closed her eyes. "He's probably with Mike and Dave, doing big boy things, Joan. How would I know?"

Dottie joined them as they were making their way out of the dining room. She grabbed her notebook from the table, and nodding to the posse, she followed Dee and Dulcie to their places on the veranda. They settled as per normal. Dulcie opened her book, Dee fished her iPod and headphones from her handbag, and Dottie withdrew her knitting from the *bilim.* They got to work.

"I wonder how much she paid those four to back her up," said Dottie, over her yellow wool.

"Looks a bit like she was expecting a battle this morning," whispered Dulcie.

Dee pulled one headphone off her ear; she'd heard the two comments quite clearly. "Fat lot of good those two in the wheelchairs and their mamby-pamby husbands would be if it really came to a fight."

Frank poked his nose around the library door and found to his surprise, the two lone wolves, Dave and Mike playing cards of a far table.

He nodded at Laurie and asked if he could join the others and Laurie said, by all means, go for it.

Frank hadn't met Dave before. He spent most of the eating hours in his room. He was short and round, with a jolly clean-shaven face, sparse grey hair, and grey eyes with long dark eye-lashes. He bared his too-white dentures as Frank sat down.

"She got you last night then," said Dave.

Frank nodded. "You heard, did you? Nightmare! Did she have a go at you, too?"

"Oh yeah," said Dave, "did she ever. 'Bout five years ago. It'd be that wouldn't it, Mike?"

"Easily mate. Mind you I get mixed up with my own little escapade with her. I had to point a gun at her to get away from me. That put the wind up 'er a bit." He cackled. Happy days!

"Mine was a bit more subtle." Dave scrunched up his button nose. "She cornered me in the dolphin garden. Came up, all cute and pouty-like and plonked herself on my lap like a 5 year old, nearly knocked me backwards off the seat. I squawked like hell, and she fled in tears. That was the last I heard of it though. She's never looked my way again. Hah!"

"Oh, that's dreadful. She took me to the dolphin garden too. Told me she needed a man, and I was just the chap! Is the woman unhinged?"

"You know what, Frank, we don't actually know. Because she owns most of this joint, we can't get a doc in to examine her, she just puts the mockers on it, says no way, and that's the end of it. I mean, she's quite clearly off her trolley, and totally sex mad."

Mike hooted. “Woman her age. Ought to be locked up!”

Frank chuckled, he’d found some friends. “What do you think I should do?”

“What’re your options, mate? You can leave, you can report her, but what would you say. She hasn’t actually raped you yet … has she?” Dave looked horrified for a moment.

“God no, of course not. Me and the Teapots had an idea, but if I tell you, you’ve got to keep mum.”

“Oh, we’re on your side, mate. We like those three old girls! No worries there,” said Mike. “What’s your plan?”

Frank recounted the episode in Dulcie’s bathroom, and the detail of the previous night’s escapade, then he outlined the plan and the boys sat open mouthed at the finale.

Dave chimed in. “Oh bugger. And I called them three old girls. Just goes to show. They’ve got some brains and spunk between them. Good on ‘em I say!”

“Well, blow me down and butter me on both sides. Who’d have thought it?” said Mike. Then thoughtfully, he said, “We’ll have to be real careful, sneaky even. She gets wind of it, she’ll do everything she can to sabotage it.”

Dave sat up and banged the table with the flat of his hands. “But it’s a bloody beautiful plan. We’ll help, won’t we, Mike?”

“Yep, whatever you need, mate. Just let us know, we’re on your side. Kindred spirits joined by past experiences.”

***

It didn’t take long for Joan to tire of her little posse. Nobody paid any attention to her, the two lone wolves weren’t even there to watch her in action; she still had a score to settle with those two. But that could wait. She dismissed the group with an imperious wave of her hand. Then, an idea percolating in her mind, she set off for the lift.

Once in her bedroom she dropped her jeans and jacket on the

floor, foraged around in her bottom drawer — her bathing suit draw — and dragged a leopard skin bikini from between the tangled strings of others bathers. Her underwear joined the other pieces on the floor, while she donned her bikini along with a rakish moleskin hat pulled down over one eye. It kept tipping off her high hair-do, so she swore at it and pulled the bee-hive to pieces. Once satisfied with the blond rats-tail strands around her face, she donned the cap again, found a bathing towel and her gold lamé sandals. Then she examined the whole in the mirror and decided it was good.

She waved a casual goodbye to the four incumbents on the wall, and took the lift to the ground floor. Skipping neatly around the back of the stairs towards the tennis court and the swimming pool, she considered checking the Library to see if 'the boys' were there. She would invite them for swim!

She was on the verge of pushing open the door to the Library when she remembered that one of them had once pointed a gun at her. She shuddered. She couldn't remember which one it was, but it had not been a nice experience. She shuddered again at the memory of her loss of bladder control during that incident. Hm! She wouldn't risk that again.

She made her way to the covered swimming pool, noticed there was no one paddling about and threw her towel on a lounger. She wondered whether they would hear her in the Library. Someone would anyway. They might think it was a suicide attempt if she did it right. Then they'd wonder who had driven her to it. Frank Chambers, of course. The dirty rotten two-timer! That'd teach him.

She waded in up to her shoulders, and felt for one moment, a sense of cool peace. The chlorinated salt water was just the right temperature. Absolutely divine. She imagined herself floating gracefully on her back, her body buoyed by the water. She bent back, waggling her feet and flapping her hands a little as she moved further into the deep end like a beautiful mermaid.

When she put her head back into the water, her cap floated

away and she made to grab it, but missed. She swore. She tried to put her feet down but discovered she was out of her depth, and her cap was disappearing towards the far end of the pool. Her heart skipped a couple of beats but she ignored its warning, rolling forward into a breast stroke position and moving her arms in the proscribed manner. The cap just kept getting further away and her blond tendrils were sticking to her face, in her eyes and her mouth. She gulped and tried to push the hair out of the way, but she missed her stroke and suddenly water was in her mouth, she inhaled rapidly only to gasp and inhale another mouthful as she floundered beneath the water's surface. She flapped her arms to reach the light, but her mouth filled with water again, and when she tried to spit it out she breathed in another great dollop of water into her lungs. Suddenly, she was sinking; panic surging through her. She fought her way up and screamed. It had been planned as a little ladylike toot, an 'oh-dear-I-think-I'm-in-trouble' squeak, but this came out as a full blown howl.

"Help! Help! I'm dro…." Gurgle. Joan's heart was beating a dangerous bongo drum in her chest, and there was no one around. "Help!" she shouted. "Help…" Her heart fluttered and stopped beating and Joan went down again.

***

Dave, Mike and Frank had just shut the Library door when they heard the last howl. Frank jogged around the corner in time to see Joan's blond mop disappearing under the waves. He threw off his shoes, drew his shirt over his head and dived in. It was not a big pool so he was beside her in seconds, her hair flowing like jellyfish tentacles up towards the surface of the pool. He grabbed the tentacles and pulled with all his might. It looked like her entire scalp had come away in his hand until he realised it was a wig, and its owner was still heading to the bottom of the pool.

He threw the wig to the side and duck-dived down, grabbing

her shoulders, and kicking frantically with both feet to reach the surface. His army training still embedded, he placed his hand under her chin and pulled her to the side. Mike and Dave grabbed an arm each and as they dragged her onto the pool steps the rubbery double padded cups of her bikini top shot out of their holders to float cheerfully away towards the cap.

They glanced at each other and nodded. An unsaid agreement that much as they disliked the woman they would keep that a secret.

She spluttered and coughed, rolled over and spewed pool water onto the paving stones. Her hair was a tangled mess hanging from the edge of the lounge chair. Her head was covered in a mass of short grey brush-like spikes. She glared at the three men, speechless. She snatched the wig from the lip of the lounge chair and pulled it over her head like a bathing cap. Then she started to cry, great whoops of sobs, torn from the depths as she buried her head in the towel Mike handed her.

The boys looked at each other and nodded again. They left her there, alone with her embarrassment. What else could they do?

"Another one to keep quiet about?" said Dave.

"Hmm," said Frank.

"I reckon," said Dave. And the three left the scene, checked their watches and nodded. It was nearly dinner time

Dinner was a dull affair, made even more so by the fact that Joan did not appear, so again they couldn't play the scene they had planned that morning.

When Sam appeared, he was beside himself. Prudence kept patting his arm and he kept snatching it away. When Frank passed him on the way to the servery, Sam hissed at him.

"What've you done with her? You're poison to her, where is she?"

Frank shook his head. "How could I possibly know, Sam?" He strode to his table as fast as his legs would carry him and laid his and

Dulcie's plates in front of them. He looked at his knees, then grabbed a serviette and covered them.

"What's the matter, darling? What's ailing you?"

Frank looked longingly at Dulcie, the other too peering at him as if a great secret was buried in his heart.

"I can't tell you. Not here anyway. I made a promise to the boys. I really can't."

"What on earth has happened? We never had secrets, Frank."

"I know darling, but this one is not only mine to keep. It belongs to another and I made a pact."

Dulcie was furious. "Not good enough, Frank Chambers. Not after all these years."

"Ssh! Dulcie, keep your voice down, otherwise your secret will be out too. If Frank can't tell you, he can't tell you. Honour his honour, woman." Dottie glared at Dulcie, and Dee scowled. She'd unplugged in time to hear the last few comments.

"I can't believe you're backing him up! What's going on here? That's it. I bet it's something to do with that bloody woman. Well, I'm done for the day, not going to have my friends turning against me, now of all times." And Dulcie grabbed her bag and her book, lurched to her feet, grabbed her cane and hobbled off into the distance.

Frank heaved a huge sigh. "What the hell do I do now?"

"Whatever it is that you can't tell us, don't worry. It'll blow over." Dottie placed her hand over Franks. "She loves you, Frank. She can't believe she's found you again after all this time. It's only natural that she wants all of you, doesn't want to share you with anyone else, least of all you know who, and certainly not anyone else's secret."

Sam didn't say much but there was nothing wrong with his hearing. He tittered and grinned into his dinner.

Dulcie went straight to her bedroom, and threw her bag on her bed. She wanted to cry. What was Frank hiding? What couldn't he tell her? She glared at the patterned carpet for a while, hating the roses more and more. Which was odd because she'd never minded them before.

She shrugged out of her clothes and headed to the bathroom. Nothing like a good soak when you're feeling miserable. She let the hot water seep into her body, soaping all over. She'd been so happy, in spite of what Joan had done. Joan would never spoil her joy but something had happened to Frank that afternoon, and he suddenly felt like a stranger. She wanted to wail.

She dried her skin with the fresh towel and reached for the talcum powder. She tipped the bottle up and shook the soft white powder into her hand, reaching under her arms and between her legs. The bathroom mirror reflected a scowling face framed by silvery, scrub-bud hair, so she tipped the talc bottle and shook it over her head making her look like a snowman. It didn't make her laugh, so she smoothed the talc over her bulges while her mind tripped back sixty-five years to when her mother would stroke her little body with talc, massaging it soothingly into her skin. She'd loved it then and was trying hard to love it now, but the events of the evening had invaded her thoughts. She pulled her pink nightie over her head and climbed in to bed.

A couple of hours later Dulcie woke with a crawling sensation on her skin as if ants were skittering all over her. She scratched. They continued skittering and she turned the light on. The white talcum powder, so soothing earlier, had clumped in all her creases and an alarming redness had developed.

She got out of bed, took off her nightie and went to the bathroom. She looked like a pink and white patchwork quilt. She scratched again under her arms and peered at her body.

She could see the flesh above her pubic hair, not something she inspected very often, and saw a dark red rash. Perhaps she had been scratching in her sleep. Did she have crabs? Oh God, the very thought made her stomach turn. How could she have got crabs? She turned the shower on, and even though it was cold at first she climbed in and let the cool water run over her body. It felt better. Ten minutes later, she was not only clean again, but cold as well. She wrapped herself in the towel she'd used earlier and inspected the damage — still pink and white and itchy, but not so bad.

She ran her eyes over the bed and saw little piles of talcum powder clinging to the sheets. She wet a finger with her tongue, and collected some from a small patch, and finding her spectacles she examined it. There were little brown flecks mixed in with the talc; she knew they'd never been there before. What on earth were they?

She ripped the sheets off the bed, opened the window, and shook them violently. She didn't have another set, they'd only just been changed; she would have to sleep on the mattress protector and hope the talc had not seeped through.

She scratched some more under her arms and then the grey tufts between her legs — that was not funny — not funny at all.

What could be in the talcum powder and how the hell had it got there? She popped her reading spectacles on again and examined some of the talcum powder flecks on the floor. She thought they were moving. She had a magnifying glass somewhere, what had she done with it? Bedside table? No. Bottom drawer of the tall boy? No. Bathroom cabinet? Ah yes, there it was. She gave it a wipe with her fresh nightie and peered at the moving mass on the floor. Bugs, bed bugs, or ants? She wanted to stamp on them all, heel them into the floor, but she realised that would just send them into the carpet and create an even bigger problem. She padded to the bathroom again and grabbed two hand towels and soaked them in a basin of water, then laid them over the white and wriggly brown patches on the carpet. That should keep the little buggers quiet for a while, she thought. But she was still itching and she realised on her next trip into the bathroom that her skin was red and raised like a rash and it would only get worse if she scratched. She knew who'd done this, she knew who'd had access to her room and she knew she couldn't call Dr Prince at this time of night for some anti-histamine cream. She would just have to suffer, but she would make plans for someone else to suffer too. This was unforgiveable.

Dulcie took a Temazepam with some water and went back to bed. I'll just have to knock myself out otherwise I'll never sleep, she thought. She'd think about retaliation in the morning.

Chapter 11

'Honestly, if you're given the choice between
Armageddon or tea, you don't say 'what kind of tea?'
Neil Gaiman

When Dulcie arrived at breakfast, looking less than sparkling, the other three were already there.

"Gee, Dulce, you could scrub up a bit now you're a Feeannsay!" chortled Dottie.

Joan was nowhere to be seen.

Dulcie scratched under her arms, and turning away from the group, scratched her itchy pubic area. She could have screamed.

"The key and cling film was not the only thing Joan did in my room." Dulcie paused, not for effect, but because she had to scratch under her chin.

"What! What?" yelled Dee, buried under her headphones.

"Take them off, Dee. How the hell do you expect to hear anything? For Gawd's sake!" Dottie pulled the headphones off Dierdre's ears.

"What, darling? What happened?" Frank said, reaching for her hand.

Both hands shot to her armpits where she scratched like a chimpanzee.

"She put bed bugs, or ants or something in my talc." Dulcie wriggled on her seat as she endeavoured to avoid scratching her privates in front of Frank.

"She did what?" the two girls chimed together.

"She put bugs or ants or something unpleasant in my talc. Itching powder. I can't stop itching."

"Oh No! No! That's the final straw. Nothing can forgive that." Dee had removed her headphones and was stifling a guffaw.

Dottie's mouth was hanging open. "That's outrageous. Oh dear, poor you!" She burst out laughing, uncontrollable mirth that quickly spread around the table; even Dulcie who was scratching every part of her body, joined in.

Frank grinned, happy in some small measure that the pressure to tell another's secrets had been deferred, at least for a while. It would have to come out sooner or later.

"Can I help? Not with the scratching, obviously. Is there something we can do? Surely there's an antidote?" he said. "Actually, I remember an antidote that Beryl used in Townsville for this sort of thing. Do you know if there's any Aloe Vera in the garden?" he said, laying his serviette on the table beside his empty plate.

"Yes. Definitely," said Dottie, "there's some in a big veggie patch. Masses of it. We drink it sometimes if we have tummy problems." She got up from the table, and took off down the garden. "Come on — not going to let this beat us!"

"Let's go! Dulcie, can you walk?" Frank put his hand on her arm.

"Yes, but I'd like some breakfast first. You carry on, I'll catch you up." She rose from the table and headed to the servery, helped herself to some bacon and eggs, tea and toast and returned to the table.

"You carry on, Frank. I'll manage."

Frank cocked his head to one side. He could see he had not yet been forgiven and probably wouldn't be until he'd told the tale, but it was clear he needed to leave her to her breakfast.

He touched her lightly on the shoulder. "I love you, Dulcie. Always have, always will."

She looked up at him with her periwinkle blue eyes, but they were not smiling. She scratched her arm and scowled.

Frank nodded and made for the garden where Dottie and Dee had disappeared. He had no idea where they'd gone and had no hope of finding the Aloe Vera patch on his own. He stood uncertain for a minute then went back into the dining room and took the seat next to Dulcie.

He cast about to see who might overhear. "Yesterday afternoon, I met Mike and Dave in the Library and they told me about their little episodes with you know who."

Dulcie looked across at him, wiping the toast crumbs from her lips. "And? Is that it? That's your special secret?"

"No. No. After we left the Library we heard screams from the pool, and Joan was in there. She'd obviously lost her footing and appeared to be drowning. She was nearly on the bottom. So I dived in and pulled her up by the hair … but her hair came off in my hand."

Dulcie's eyes grew round and she put a hand to her mouth in a silent, 'Oh.'

"I grabbed her under the shoulders and pulled her to the side. She lost half the pool when she coughed it all up, then was wild with fury when she saw she'd lost her wig and it was lying on the chair. Even worse all the padding from her bikini top had come out and was floating across the pool, like little boats. She was so angry, she didn't even thank us for saving her. That's why we promised to keep it a secret for her sake. But now she's done this to you, with the bugs, I'm of a mind not to keep her secret anymore."

"Oh Frank. For goodness sake, what was she thinking? Playing the damsel in distress? In a bikini, at her age. Dear Lor! And then you went in and saved her. You'll never hear the end of it now … one way or another. You'll be her knight in shining armour but with a terrible secret to boot. It'll make the whole thing even worse." She scratched under her arm and rose from the table.

"Let's go and find this Aloe Vera, the girls will have got it by now. If I walk I can scratch all sorts of places you can't even begin to see or imagine — all at once!" She rolled her bottom around wiggling her hips and rubbing her knees against each other. Frank laughed; he loved this woman so much, she was never fazed for long.

Dulcie led him through the winding maze to a part of the garden Frank hadn't seen before. A huge area filled with veggies and tropical fruit trees. One bed was dedicated to Aloe Vera. Dee was already down on her hands and knees, breaking off the prickly leaves that were plump with juice.

"Here, Dot, put these in your skirt — make a basket."

Frank knelt to help and soon Dottie's skirt basket was full to bursting.

"I'm going to turn into a pin cushion if I put any more in here," said Dottie. "That'll do to start with. We just have to get it back without being seen. They'll have a fit if they catch us nicking stuff from the veggie patch. Frank, you go ahead and keep a look out. You all right, Dulce, you look like you're going to explode."

"I haven't got enough hands. If I don't get this sorted soon, I might very well turn into a gorilla." She scratched under arms, and then taking advantage of Frank's back being turned, attacked her pubic mound with the heel of her hand.

"Sure she didn't put crabs in your talc, Dulce?" said Dee with only the shadow of a grin. She was trying hard to keep herself in check, very glad she wasn't the butt of the pranks. She'd be plotting murder if it'd been her; Dulcie was so much nicer a person, she'd never consider murder — not yet anyway.

***

Joan caught the procession as it made its way up the lawn, but she was hardly in the mood to be amused. Her fuzz-covered head itched from the salt chlorine in the pool, and she'd hung her saturated blond wig on a head stand on her dressing table. She was determined to retrieve the padding from her bikini top but knew she would have to time it right. Make sure everyone was at lunch or their afternoon naps. The Teapots would be occupied for a while, that was for sure.

She opened her wardrobe door and chose yet another wig from yet another head stand on the top shelf of the cupboard. The black Mary Quant-style bob she'd bought the other day in Cairns would do nicely. She was wracked with a mixture of emotions: embarrassment at her failed prank, gratitude for Frank's gallantry and absolute fury at having been seen by Mike and Dave. They would never keep it quiet, she'd be the laughing stock of the Home. She'd have to do something to take attention away from her stupidity. Maybe Frank was keen on her after all. It had been his daring that had saved her life. She didn't want to think about the fact that she had nearly drowned, all because of that stupid cap. Where was the bloody thing, anyway? Oh Damn, it's still in the pool with my bra pads. She threw on some casual lounge clothes and grabbed her posy basket. She'd look like she was off to pick flowers.

***

Frank crossed the lawn first, checking in all directions, except up, in case a member of staff appeared. Dottie and her basket followed Frank, with Dee and Dulcie flanking her. He left the girls to it when they reached Dulcie's room, taking her in his arms saying he would see her at lunch and wishing her luck.

In the room they noticed the bed had been remade with fresh sheets. On her way to the dining room for breakfast Dulcie had mentioned to Madge that she'd had yet another accident, and Madge, gentle as ever, had assured her the matter would be taken care of.

Dottie took charge. "I think we're going to make a mess of these sheets too, Dulce. How do you want to do this?" she passed some of the Aloe Vera leaves to Dierdre. "Here, you start squeezing, and we'll make a paste. You know what would be good, one of those spaghetti presses. You know, like they use to make lasagna. I'll go down to the kitchen. Sarah will have one."

She was back in ten minutes. Dulcie had undressed to her undies and bra; she still looked like a pink and white tablecloth.

"Oh God, Dulce, you poor old thing. Look at you!" Dottie gave Dulcie a hug; this was not a nice thing. "Guess who I just saw?"

"Who?" Dulcie and Dee said at the same time.

"Her! The mad woman! Coming out of the kitchen. She screamed at me. She's gone nuts!"

"What did she say?"

"She said, 'what's the matter with your friend — she got crabs? He'll never want her now. How could she ever think he'd like her more than me?' Then she did that hyena laugh thing she does. Woman's insane."

Dulcie lay on the bed after they'd stripped off the sheets, and the girls started covering her with the jelly that Dottie had squeezed out with the lasagne maker. It worked well. In no time at all, Dulcie looked like a moss blanket. The other side was more of a challenge.

"Here, I'll just rub it all in — feels nice actually, very soothing. I haven't got much of a rash on my back I don't think. Just the backs of my legs and my bum."

"Ok, right. Roll over and we'll do your back." Dee helped Dulcie to turn over without slopping too much of the still glossy jelly over everything, and applied it to her legs.

"You do your bum, Dulce. Not going there. Hah!" Dee said. "I hope no one comes in. This would be hard to explain!"

There was a knock on the door.

"Oh Gawd! Who is it?" Dulcie shouted upside down.

"It's just me." Frank whispered. "Are you coming for lunch?"

"Not just yet, Frank. A little indisposed at the mo!" Dulcie turned to Dottie. "Tell him what we're doing, Dot."

Dottie went to the door and whispered through the crack. "Can't come in, Frank. Dulcie's upside down in an aloe patch. Go on down, we'll join you shortly."

"OK, see you down there!"

"How do I get to lunch with this stuff all over me?" Dulcie had a good point.

"Maybe this is one you sit out. We can bring something up for you," said Dottie.

"Good idea, then I can let it soak in a bit. It feels good. Cooling."

"Ok, then, see you later. Soak nicely!" Dottie and Dierdre washed and dried their hands then closed the door behind them.

Dulcie lowered herself on to the bed again, and after rubbing the aloe into the itchy bits on the back of her legs and her bottom she rolled over.

She wished Frank were there to smooth the aloe into her skin. His hands had always been so gentle. No one had ever touched her like he had. She wondered if he still would, whether his past, and his horrific injuries would hinder their love. As a couple in their seventies, should they expect to be able to make love like before? Doubtful, but there were things they could do. Good heavens, she thought, I haven't even considered anything like that since Bob died. Would she still be able to … accommodate?

She massaged the aloe jelly into her skin, enjoying the slowness, the not hurrying; the cool sensation was getting warmer by the minute. As was she! Her thoughts were scampering, memories lighting the skies of her mind. She and Frank had been very good together. Could they be again?

A knock on the door whisked her back to reality.

"Hold on," she yelled, throwing a dressing gown over her underwear.

She opened the door.

"Here's some lunch. Guess what it is. Ham, salad and tiny, tinned potatoes." Dottie chuckled, squeezing through the door.

She placed the plate on the side table by Dulcie's chair and plonked herself onto the bed. She ran her hand over the mattress cover. The pale green aloe film was still sticky and glutinous to the touch.

"Looks like this'll need changing again too, Dulce. They're going to start wondering what's going on up here!"

"I know. I'll pop down and tell them shortly; they can get it done before tonight, I hope."

"So — no Joan at lunch. Samuel furious. Had another go at Frank. It's all his fault of course, poor bugger! Prudence had a crying fit and dropped all her pills on the floor under the table, and then started screaming that there was an infestation of cockroaches in the dining room. It took Sarah and Lisa ten minutes to calm her down and pick up all her little brown pills. It's a laugh a week down there darlin'. You're better off up here."

"Where's Frank now?"

"Not sure. He said he had an appointment — maybe he went to buy you an engagement ring!" Dottie gave a short cackle, then reached for Dulcie and gave her a hug.

"It'll all work out darlin', don't you worry! We'll sort Joan out. She can't go on doing this sort of thing forever. Sooner or later she'll give up."

Chapter 12

'Remember the tea kettle – it is always
up to its neck in hot water, yet it still sings!'
Anon

Frank knocked on the surgery door; it was out of normal consulting hours, but he hoped he might catch the doctor in his break.

The door opened and a tousled Pamela Evans smiled, pushing her long hair behind her ears.

"Hello, Frank. Sorry, we're closed at the moment. Is it urgent?"

"Yes, sort of. Any chance of a quick word with the doc?"

"Hold on. I'll go and see if he can spare a minute."

Frank caught a quick glimpse of her skirt caught up in her knickers as she walked away.

Frank grinned. Not the best timing then — he thought Dr Prince was 'seeing' Madge, at least that's what it had looked like at the beach excursion. Maybe he was playing in both camps. The old dog!

"Frank, hello!" Dr Prince opened the door wide and gestured for Frank to come in. "Sorry, my friend, little lunchtime siesta. You know! What can I do for you? Everything all right?"

Frank entered the surgery, noting the absence of Pamela but an abundance of magazines all over the floor. Dr Prince bent to pick them up as if he did it every day.

"Come on in, my friend," he said, showing him in to the consulting room. Frank wondered if the doc thought that making a friend of him would ensure his silence. With what Frank was about to tell him, it probably would.

He settled into the chair and grinned at the doctor. "You were right about Joan. She's making life very difficult. She's trying to warn Dulcie off me and me off her." Frank paused still wondering if this was a good idea. "What she doesn't know is that Dulcie and I knew each other fifty years ago. We were engaged to be married before I was called up. But then we lost touch. The only way we can think of to stop Joan is for me to announce my intention to marry Dulcie."

"Ah! I see the problem. And we don't have room for another married couple so that would mean you both being turned out on the street. Or, keeping it secret until a solution can be found or one of the other couples drops off the perch. So to speak. Sorry, awful thing to say. Ha! Ha!"

"Well, yes! But I want to be with Dulcie; we've waited fifty years. I don't want to hide it forever just because that hyena wants what she wants."

"Ha! Good one, hyena. Yes, the laugh. I get it. Has Dulcie agreed — to marry you I mean," said Dr Prince rubbing his index finger up and down the side of his nose.

"Oh yes, absolutely. I'd like to buy her an engagement ring. And, I'd like to be able to … er… consummate our engagement … again! We were very good together way back when, but I was … damaged during the war and I might be a bit compromised in that area. Any suggestions?"

"Right. Now, that's something we can take care of straight away." The doctor swivelled his chair and delved into a drawer behind him, pulling out a little packet of blue pills.

"Here! A quarter or maybe a half is the usual amount — you'll have to experiment. If it's simply a muscular atrophy issue these will do the job. Lots of fun experimenting anyway!"

Frank popped the packet in his pocket.

"Now, as for the other issue — I did warn you. I would avoid her as much as possible. She's already killed one of our residents with her persistence; we don't want to lose another one. Trouble is, there's little I can do to stop her, unless she gets violent; has she done anything like that?"

Frank told him about the glad wrap over the toilet seat, the itching powder and the missing key, but didn't mention the swimming pool incident.

"Let's keep an eye on it then. Let me know if anything else happens and if it does, I'll have a chat with Paul Longley. Keep mum for the moment though, best of luck. Let me know how you go with th ... well, maybe not … you'll know what to do!" He led Frank to the door. Pamela was in place behind the reception desk looking neat and tidy, and Frank grinned at her on the way out.

He went in search of Dulcie. Itching and aloe juice or not, he needed to talk to her and then if she was willing, introduce her to the packet of blue. As he walked past the pool he caught sight of a tall black-haired person leaning over the water. He carried on reading the instructions on the packet imagining it was only a gardener cleaning the pool until a shrill call alerted him to his mistake.

"Oh, Frank, Frank," she whinnied, galloping to his side. "I've been looking for you everywhere."

Frank stuffed the packet back into his pocket, but she was too quick for him. She giggled and laid her basket full of cap and bra pads on the ground beside her. "What's that you're hiding, Frank?" She grabbed the leaflet from his hand, holding it up to the light. Even a blind horse could've read the letters: VIAGRA.

"Oh Frank, you are so sweet, so thoughtful. Who'd have thought you'd do this for me, your gallantry knows no bounds. I am so embarrassed after my silly accident this morning, I don't know how I can thank you?"

"There's no need to thank me, Joan, anyone would have done the same."

"Oh no, Mike and Dave didn't, did they? Only you. And now this." She reached into his pocket in one swift move and pulled the packet from its hiding place. "You're such a gentleman. I keep telling Samuel that you are such a gentleman, he should take a leaf from your book."

Frank reached for the packet but Joan whisked it away, grinning coyly.

"I'll keep them in my room, darling. Then they'll always be in the right place when we need them. I knew you cared, Frank. I just knew! Oh, I'm sooo excited." And she licked his cheek. "Tonight, my Frank. Tonight, we will consummate our love."

Frank remained rooted to the spot as she skipped away. He wiped her slobber off his face, found a seat in the lounge and sat down hard on it.

He had to find Dulcie. And he had to get that packet back. Or, get another one. He shook his head in despair, and headed back to the surgery, just catching Dr Prince on his way out the door.

"Hello again, Frank. You use those up already, mate – you old stud? Hah!"

"Sort of. Well, no obviously not. She, Joan, caught me reading the instructions and thought they were for her. Now I'm in deep doo-doo. She thinks I'm going to her room tonight to do the deed. Could you give me another packet so I can at least … er … talk to Dulcie about it?"

"Oh dear! That'd be funny if it wasn't so awful! Here, take these. I always carry a couple of spares around with me — just in case, you know, someone like yourself, has a need!" He scuttled off, chuckling away.

Frank carried on through the lounge but no Teapots were in sight. Gentle snoring could be heard as pages of newspaper fluttered in the breeze made by snoozing geriatrics. No one saw him as he walked through the dining room and up the stairs to his room. A pink piece of paper poked a triangle out from the door. He opened the note.

‘I LOVE YOU FRANK. I‘LL MAKE YOU SO HAPPY. WE’LL BE PERFECT TOGETHER. LET’S DO IT TONIGHT — 6PM IN MY ROOM — NO. 5 THIRD FLOOR. LET’S NOT BOTHER WITH DINNER, WE CAN EAT EACH OTHER INSTEAD.’

Frank bolted to his bathroom and threw up in the basin. And again. He ran the tap to sluice the vomit down the drain then washed his face and wiped his hands. He peered at himself in the mirror and shook his head. He folded the note and was about to put it in the waste bin when he thought better of it. It was evidence; better kept under lock and key.

He went to the wardrobe where he pulled out the battered brown suitcase. He pushed the note into the bottom of it, slammed the lid down and put it back in the wardrobe.

He sat on his bed, realising with a wry smile that he hardly noticed the awful wallpaper anymore. The handy man hadn’t yet showed up to paint the room but somehow the presence of Dulcie had put the nightmare pictures out of his mind. He stowed the two new blue tablets in the bathroom cabinet, and feeling happy that the room was tidy and clean, went along the corridor to find Dulcie. He knocked but there was no reply. He knocked again but still nothing. Perplexed, he headed downstairs.

***

Dulcie approached the reception desk. “Madge, hello dear. I’m so sorry to do this again, but I’ve had yet another accident upstairs and I managed to save the new sheets but the mattress protector has suffered.” Dulcie liked Madge, she’d always been kind to her, and Dulcie had returned the favour.

“Well now Dulcie, you know that after three accidents I have to report it to Dr Prince.”

“Yes, I know, but they weren’t really accidents actually, more incidents that involved some unfortunateness — on the sheets. Do you have to report it?"

"In principal, yes, I do." Madge patted Dulcie's sun-spotted hand. "It's that or tell Major Longley — it's about the cost of the laundry you see."

"Oh, yes, I see." Dulcie nibbled a knuckle. "Look, it's not a disaster, I can do without the mattress protector until the next time, would that be better?"

"Why don't you want me to tell Dr Prince, Dulcie? Wouldn't it be better, so he could help you?"

"Ah well, it's not one of those problems you see. And I don't want to get anyone into trouble. Look, don't worry, I'll just cope, it's not smelly or anything, nothing like last time. Don't worry, Madge. Forget I mentioned it!"

Dulcie smiled her thanks, and turning away from the desk wandered through the lounge into the dining room. It wasn't close to the dinner hour, yet the tables were being laid. She wondered what delights the kitchen had in store for them tonight. Ham and soggy lettuce perhaps, again.

She looked around the lounge, most of the residents had gone up to their rooms, either to change or lie down. She wandered out to the garden where the light was darkening as storm clouds were gathering over the mountains. They couldn't see the ocean from Rosehill, but they knew where it was. The westerly direction was where the evening sunlight came from to kiss the handkerchief bushes of the maze. It was all rainforest covered mountains, dense and dangerous. Only once had she taken a stroll in there when she first arrived several years ago. Terry Maidens had been alive then, before Joan frightened him to death, and he'd taken her for a walk through the jungle showing her the plants that could harm: the stinger bush, so pretty to look at, furry heart-shaped leaves with serrated edges, pink bell like flowers, and tiny silica hairs that stick in your skin and inject a neurotoxin into your blood stream that is so painful that some people had chosen suicide rather than try to bear it. Soldiers from the pioneer days had mistakenly used the leaves for toilet paper, and paid the price with their own bullet. Then there was the wait-a-while vine or lawyer cane, so called because once it got its hooks into your skin you had the devil of a job tearing it free — just like a lawyer. Or Joan for that matter.

Dulcie had enjoyed the walk, had even quite liked Terry, but although she'd been widowed a couple of years by then, she wasn't ready for anything new. And, of course, Joan had been there; ready to pounce on the poor man when he least expected it. He hadn't lasted long. Dulcie had felt sad for him at the time, but perhaps getting involved with Joan would have been worse. She hoped that her own engagement to Frank would put Joan off the scent for good, but she had her doubts.

Where was Frank anyway, she thought? Maybe she should find him and reassure him that she was fine, now the Aloe Vera had almost done its job.

The first crack of lightning heralded the rumble of thunder which soon rolled over the horizon, and turning from the garden she hurried in. The staff was well prepared and the chairs and umbrellas had already been taken into the lounge. Her watch showed 5.45pm; people would be arriving for dinner soon.

The first person she saw was Dr Prince, not someone who usually joined them in the evening. He was hurrying towards her, an unusual expression on his face.

"Dulcie, Dulcie, I need a word. Please — come over here." He pulled her arm and she followed him into the alcove near the dining room toilets — the alcove from which she had seen Frank for the first time in fifty years. She followed Dr Prince, curiosity and dread spiking her heart rate.

"Dulcie, I'm sorry to jump you like this but I think you should know. Frank could be in for a spot of bother. He came to me this afternoon with a delicate matter to discuss — mum's the word of course, but congratulations — but the other issue has gone a bit awry and Joan Holloway-Potts-Jones has caught wind of it and is planning an assault this evening."

"An assault? Hold on, I've no idea what you're talking about. The first thing — I'm guessing at, and yes, thanks. But I don't know what you mean by another issue gone awry."

"I think the best thing would be for you to go to Frank's room and make sure he doesn't leave. I'll cover for you in case … you know …"

"No, I don't know what you're talking about. But I was looking for him anyway, so let's go." Dulcie set off towards the lift. Her cane no longer featured in her attire; she hadn't needed it for days.

Frank's room, No. 23, was only five doors away from Dulcie's. She hadn't realised they were so close. Dr Prince knocked.

"Frank! Mr Chambers? It's Dr Prince."

No response.

"Frank, it's Dulcie, can we come in?"

Still no response. They looked at each other.

"Perhaps we missed him if the lift and stairs crossed. I'll go down and see. You stay here in case he comes back up. He's probably looking for you, too."

Dulcie wasn't comfortable standing outside Frank's room so she headed back to her own. She'd wait just inside her door and catch him when he came back up the stairs.

But her door was locked. That's odd she thought. She knew she hadn't locked it, perhaps Madge had asked the cleaning staff to change her mattress protector after all.

Her thoughts were interrupted when Frank and Dr Prince appeared at the top of the stairs. They turned left to Frank's room.

Dulcie trotted back along the corridor as Frank unlocked his door. "Come on in," he said, holding the door wide.

Dr Prince indicated for Dulcie to go in first. It was many years since she'd been in that room; Mavis's old room. Not since Mavis had become bedridden and refused visitors. It looked the same but smelled different — thankfully. Frank indicated for them to sit down.

Dr Prince spoke first. “Look, I don't need to be here to help you with this problem, but just let me say that I’m on your side. I’ve seen what Joan can do when she sets her mind on something, or someone, so you have my sympathies. Your secret is safe with me and I suggest that you both stay here until the danger has passed.”

“What danger? What on earth is going on? You two are playing secret squirrels and I’ve no idea what you are talking about.”

Dr Prince looked at Frank who nodded, giving him permission to go ahead. “Frank came to see me earlier and told me what Joan’s been up to. He also told me you are engaged to be married after a fifty year wait — congratulations, wonderful news — but tricky as we have no rooms available for another couple, so we need to keep it secret. Do you want to tell Dulcie the next bit?”

Frank peered at Dulcie and shrugged, embarrassed. “I also asked for some help on a personal matter and he gave me some tablets.” Dulcie flushed. “I’m sorry, my darling, but we have talked about it a bit and you know what I'm referring to. Anyway, I was reading the instructions and that bloody woman walked straight into me, saw what I was reading, and grabbed the tablets out of my pocket thinking they were for her to use ... with me. Then she left a note under my door.” He rose and went to the wardrobe, glad he hadn’t shredded the note. He pulled it from the brown leather case and handed it to Dulcie.

Dulcie turned pale as she read the note. “Oh my god, this is awful! What are we going to do?”

Dr Prince piped up. “My suggestion would be to stay here, get some dinner sent up and lay low until the night is over.”

“But what about the rules of no visiting for… you know, men and women?”

“Why don’t you both order dinner individually, and then Frank, you go to Dulcie's room, just in case Joan tries to find you in yours. I'll cover for you if anyone raises a question."

"OK. Sounds like a plan. What do you think, darling?" Frank took Dulcie's hand.

"I think that's best. But my room's locked again and I haven't got a key. I know I left it open but I'll go downstairs and get the spare. And I'll order some dinner at the same time. Thank you for your help Doctor, we can't thank you enough." Dulcie rose and headed for the door. Dr Prince held it for Dulcie, and nodded goodbye to Frank. "Best of luck."

At reception Dulcie sighed. "I'm so sorry Madge but my room's locked again. Have the cleaners been in?"

"No, dear. I haven't had time to organise it, and you did say not to worry about it."

"Yes, I did, I know. It's so strange though. I know I didn't lock it earlier when I left. I'm sorry, but could I borrow your key again and bring it back later. Oh, and could I get some dinner sent up to me? I'm not feeling the best tonight."

"Yes, of course, what would you like? A plate of ham and salad with a couple of nice little potatoes?" She giggled. "Actually I think it's cottage pie and peas tonight, just for a change!"

"What? Some relief from the norm? Thanks, Madge, you're an angel."

Madge handed her the key, and Dulcie started for the stairs. She didn't see Madge's worried expression. Madge had always liked Dulcie but she could see that things were getting too hard for the old girl, and Madge was sad it had come to that.

On the spur of the moment Dulcie changed direction and went into the dining room spying Dottie and Dierdre sitting at their table.

"Hello. We were wondering where you were."

"Listen girls, I can't talk now. I'm having dinner in my room tonight. I'll tell you all about it tomorrow."

"Oh yes, really? On your little ownsome darlin', or

accompanied perhaps?" Dottie laughed so hard she started coughing and bent double over her plate. Dee stroked her back and smiled.

Dulcie looked around the room and noticed that Joan wasn't there.

Dave Meldrum entered the room with Pamela Evans on his arm. His smile suggested conquest, but her face was devoid of excitement, or the emotion of first love. Dulcie intuited that a move had been made but had not yet been successful. Best of luck to them, she thought. They were only about thirty years apart in age, but nobody cares about that these days.

She gave Dottie's back a stroke, kissed her on the head, patted Dee's shoulder and left the dining room.

She unlocked her door with some trepidation, and looked around the room, fully expecting to see another horror. But everything seemed in order. She had already put the sheets back over the bare mattress and nothing had changed there. She sighed. If Joan was imagining herself in a night of passion with Frank it might just keep her quiet for a while, but what would happen when Frank didn't turn up? She laid the spare room key on her bedside table; *The Affair* was still there, barely disturbed, and she looked around the room checking for tidiness. After all a visitor was due, a special visitor. Perhaps this would be the night to tell him; perhaps the opportune moment would present itself.

A quiet tap at the door drew her away from the bed. She went to the door, opened it and invited Frank in.

Once she had closed and locked the door with the key, Frank took her in his arms.

She melted into him, a million memories lighting her mind. It had been so long.

"Frank, there's something I must tell you," she began.

"Not now sweetheart, later. Right now I have something to tell you." He kissed her gently on her lips and pulled her down to the edge of the bed.

"I love you, Dulcie Thomson, oh Dooley, whatever. I have always loved you and will always love you. This time I will make you my wife in name and in law. But right now, more than anything in the world, I want to make you my lover — again. Will you come with me?"

Dulcie smiled, the gentle smile of affection for the man she had adored and lost and now found again. "Yes, Frank. Definitely, yes. Should we have a little shower do you think?"

"I think we should." He took her hand and they moved to the bathroom. "Would it be alright if I undressed first? I want to show you my scars; show you that my body is not the same as it was."

She gazed at him as he removed his shirt and shorts. She saw first the scar across his belly and then the cleft under his collarbone. She touched it carefully, not sure if it would be sensitive.

"Do they hurt?"

"No, my darling, not anymore." She noticed the streaks of shiny tissue that marked the massive damage to his legs.

"Oh Frank, this must've been dreadful. My poor love."

He held her to him. His blue boxer shorts sat snug on his hips, a small paunch pushing the elastic down below his belly button. His chest, so thickly covered in black hair before, was now peppered with white contrasting the olive skin that spoke of his Italian heritage.

"Frank, I'm nervous. I look so different, I'm not…"

He placed a slender finger on her mouth and followed it with the softest of kisses. He wriggled her blouse up over her head and she lifted her arms like a child for its mother.

He kissed her neck and throat with tiny pecks and she squirmed in delight. It had been so long, and her earlier thoughts when she'd smoothed the aloe vera gel over her body came flooding back.

He stood away from her, and pulled the automatic water tap release on the shower. The water gushed from the rose, warm and welcoming.

He stepped out of his boxers and turned immediately to the shower. The water pulsed over his head.

"Come."

Dulcie nervously stepped out of her skirt, desperately wanting to keep her knickers on, wanting to hide the appendix scar but knowing that was silly. That was just one scar among many, and this man had known every inch of her body in years gone by. She let her undies drop on the floor and stepped into the shower.

He kissed her mouth, her ears, her nose and her chin, and she responded with her hands, exploring his back and his chest, hesitant to go further, but feeling through the closeness that all was well in that area. She took him in her hands, cupping him and kissing him back with increasing fervour as the warm water soaked them both and washed away their reserve.

A loud ruckus drowned the sound of the shower. Someone was screaming outside the room, banging repeatedly on the door. A key was plunged into the keyhole and they could hear the sounds of fruitless turning.

"Oh, dear God!"

"Ssh, my darling. Maybe she'll go away."

A tray and a plate of dinner hit the door with a crash, accompanied by a high-pitched screech.

"I know you're in there, Frank Chambers. You filthy two-timer. And you, Dulcie de-witch Dooley. You'll never get away with it. I'll get you for this. I'll tell everyone — everyone!"

More crashing followed, and a second dinner splattered across the timber door. Cutlery hit the floor with a clatter and then high-heeled shoes stomped off along the corridor.

Dulcie got out of the shower and reached for a towel. She was shaking. Frank followed her out, grabbing another smaller one and took her in his arms.

"It's alright darling, it's over. She knows now. She can do no more harm."

"You think so? Now is when she's at her most dangerous, Frank. Now is when she can do the most harm. She's been denied, thwarted — remember what we learned at school? *Hell hath no fury like a woman scorned.* She's been scorned and she will do everything she can to destroy us. What has gone before was merely child's play."

They sat in Dulcie's guest chairs. She'd boiled the kettle, and although they both could've done with something stronger, they sipped tea and ate ginger biscuits. Their dinner was gone. It had decorated the corridor and the door. They'd done their best to clean it up, pushing the debris into her waste bin. It would be putrid by the morning, but then she could take it downstairs and empty it into the kitchen dustbins.

"I'll head back to my room soon. I hope we can pick this up later. Oh, that's sounds ridiculous. You know what I mean, my darling. I wish someone would just get rid of her for a day, or more, and give us some peace."

"It'll be alright. Eventually. I think I'll go to bed now too. I wish we could be together."

They said goodnight at her door as she closed it softly behind him.

Two minutes later a knock surprised her.

"Yes?"

"It's me. This you have to see. You won't believe what she's done!"

Dulcie grabbed her dressing gown and followed Frank into the corridor.

When they got to his room, she gasped. "Oh, good lord." She stepped into the room and looked around her. Along the walls, great gouges of wallpaper had been ripped as if a wild animal had been through it.

"How did she get in? She must have a key to your room too?" Dulcie said.

"She must have got one from somewhere — but look…" Frank went to one wall and pulled at one of the scratches. It came off in his hand leaving the wallpaper unmarked.

"What?" Dulcie followed him to the wall and pulled at another 'scratch'. It came off in her hand.

"Yes, but look at this. Looks like she got bored with her little game and went berserk. These ones are real." Frank pulled at another scratch and the wallpaper peeled off in a long streak, then another, and another. "She's used those dreadful fake nails, or one of the dining room knives perhaps." The scratches went diagonally, horizontally and vertically, all over the walls on both sides of the room. Only the doorway and window wall had escaped.

Dulcie sank on to Frank's bed. "She's demented, Frank. She's gone completely round the twist. What should we do?"

"We'll need to get the room redecorated, that's for sure. Madge'll think I did this on purpose. She knows I hate the wallpaper."

"Why do you hate it so much darling? What's wrong with it?"

Frank looked at Dulcie, love and pain battling for supremacy. He patted the bed and she moved closer.

"When I was in hospital in Townsville ... are you sure you want to hear this?"

"Yes, of course my darling. There'll never be any secrets between us, ever again."

"Townsville — the hospital — is mostly a blur, but certain things remain pinned like darts to my memory. Every time I had another operation — mostly to fix up my legs — I went to this horrible place in my head. I think it was the withdrawal from the anaesthetic. All I could see were the blooms of blood on my soldiers' bodies as they died. They looked like huge rose petals, and it made me shake like I had the palsy. But the worse thing, if that wasn't bad enough, was the smell."

"The smell? What was the smell? You don't have to go through this if you don't want to."

"No, no, you were right. No secrets. No stone left unturned, nothing left unsaid." Frank continued. "The smell — was like roses. It was as if they filled the breathing mask with rose oil, or the nurses wore rose perfume. It was everywhere. It gave me a headache — a migraine — and every time I smell it now, I'm back there. Even the roses on the wallpaper here sent me into a panic when I first arrived. It sounds so pathetic, but I can't explain the nightmares. They just go with roses."

Dulcie held his hand. "What's odd is that I have been getting more and more annoyed at the roses in my room. How could I have picked that up from you?"

"We've been connected ever since the day you stamped on my heel with those stiletto shoes of yours. It's not surprising if we're reconnecting like that again now."

He stroked her hand and cocked his head. "What's odd is that I'm starting to get used to the wallpaper. I've stopped seeing it. And now she's ripped it, I'm seeing it again, but it almost makes me laugh, as if she's destroyed my nightmare. How bizarre is that?"

"You mean she might just have done something good without even realising it?"

"Weird isn't it?" he chuckled. "She would never know. How could she?"

"What should we do — about this?"

"Nothing tonight, that's for sure. I wish you could stay here with me. Or even me with you, but perhaps we've had enough excitement for one night. Oh, what was it you wanted to tell me?"

"Never mind about that now darling, another time, another day. It can wait." Dulcie got to her feet. "Will you sleep?"

"I believe I just might tonight, Dulcie, I believe I actually might. There has been a sort of exorcism in here. It's odd, but I feel rather relieved. Shall I see you at breakfast?"

"Yes, breakfast, of course … breakfast."

Frank took Dulcie into his arms and held her tight. He kissed her forehead and pressed his lips into her hair.

"I'll see you in the morning. Sleep well, if you can."

Dulcie closed the door behind her, her last look at the ruined wallpaper imprinted on her mind.

She threw her dressing gown on her bed and brushed her teeth, peering at herself in the mirror. What was her life coming to? She couldn't think of anything more wonderful than having Frank back but dear God, it hadn't been an easy road so far. She turned to the toilet, pulled her undies down and sat. Content and quiet for a minute. Urination! The best nation in the world! She chuckled. Automatically, she pulled at the toilet roll. Nothing happened. She turned to look at it. It didn't look quite right. She pulled again. Nothing happened. She got up, irritated, gave herself a little shake, pulled her undies up, went back into her bedroom, grabbed her glasses off the bed and entered the bathroom, again. She peered at the toilet roll. There was no front or back, no over the front rolling and no underneath rolling. They were joined. She tore at one side and pulled hard, and slowly the roll ripped and unraveled. She could tell this hadn't happened by itself. No toilet roll was made like that.

Joan!

That's why the door had been locked when she'd come back from talking to Frank and Dr Prince. That's why she'd had to go and get the key again. That's why Joan had had a key to try and unlock the door but she couldn't because it had been locked from the inside.

Beyond a joke. Way beyond a joke.

Dulcie didn't sleep a wink. At two o'clock, she got up. Her mind had kept her tossing all night. She took a tablet, half a Temazepan. She knew she'd be fuzzy in the morning, but better that than not sleeping at all. If only they could have just one day without her!

Chapter 13

'You can never get a cup of tea large enough or a book long enough to suit me.'
C.S. Lewis

Dulcie woke with a head so sore she didn't think she could make it to breakfast. Her neck was all twisted and she realised she'd slept, when she had slept, in a very awkward position. She considered asking the kitchen for breakfast upstairs, but knew that would leave Frank at Joan's mercy if he were in the dining room on his own. She couldn't expect the Teapots to handle that. And anyway they'd want to know what had happened last night. She had no secrets from Dottie and Dee, she would tell them for sure.

She staggered to the shower. Their loving the night before prompted an adrenalin thump in her nether regions. She blushed at the thought, and quietly hoped they would have a rematch soon. She chuckled at her shyness, but felt more comfortable now he'd seen her naked, and not been shocked. The water was hot and soothing and slowly her neck untwisted as she massaged the muscles under the heat.

She dressed slowly, checking her skin for rashes, and saw they'd nearly all gone. She donned a simple pink blouse and grey skirt, and brushed her corkscrew hair into obedience; it had only become wiry since it had turned grey. She could do nothing with it.

She took the lift downstairs, and took her cane with her. She hadn't needed it for days but today she felt wobbly. The dining room was full. Several residents were there who hadn't been present for weeks. Dulcie wondered if they'd heard the noise the night before, and were coming out of the woodwork to get the gossip. Joan was at the servery with her back to Dulcie. No Frank. The Teapots sat, as usual, in their rightful places; Dottie's knitting over an empty plate and Dierdre buried in her headphones.

"Whoa! Look who's here then!" said Dottie, parking her knitting. "Or should I say, look what the cat dragged in through a hedge backwards. Dear God, woman what did you get up to last night?"

"How long you got?" She sat in her usual seat.

Dottie chuckled and elbowed Dee. "Oi, Dee, get your head out of there. Dee, DEE?" Dee's face lifted and noticing Dulcie, she ripped the headphones off her ears and leant forward.

"What! What? What's been going on? You look bloody awful this morning, madam, if I may say. You been up all night have you? Hard at it?" Dee squawked with glee and slapped her hands on the table making all the crockery and cutlery jump.

"What've you heard?"

"Well now nothing much! Bloody racket at midnight. Joan gone berserk apparently. Other than that, no details — come on, out with it!"

"Suffice to say — Joan thought she had a date with Frank last night. He didn't turn up. He came to me instead. She went berserk outside my room, threw our dinner trays at the door, went to Frank's room and tore the paper off the walls with a knife — that about covers it!"

"You didn't get any dinner then?" Dee chortled. "Get anything else? Eh? Eh?"

"Ssh! Shut up, Dee," said Dottie, catching Dulcie's expression. "What else?"

"When I went to the loo, later, Joan had glued the toilet paper up so I couldn't unroll it, so I had to do the old 'shakin' Stevens' routine before I could get my specs and see what she'd done. She's still got the key but she couldn't get in when Frank and I were there, because I'd locked it from the inside, but she'd been in before. It's all getting a bit much."

"'Bout time you told someone I reckon, darlin'," said Dottie.

"Frank told Dr Prince what's been going on, and he's on our side." Dulcie got up to go to the servery to get some breakfast.

Joan turned around at the same time.

Silence.

"You think you've won, don't you Miss Clever de-witch Dooley!" Joan snorted.

"It's not a game, Joan…"

"Oh, yes it is. And it's a game you can never win! Who do you think you are? He loves me, not you. He's just playing you along, because you're easy. Hah! Easy meat! Always have been. Even with Terry Maidens — easy pickings. Anyway, I saw him first."

Dulcie flushed red and furious. She was not in the mood. "I don't think so, Joan. You certainly did not see him first. I knew him fifty years ago. Fifty years ago in Brisbane. We were at University together. And, we were engaged to be married before the Vietnam War took him away. And — we're engaged to be married again. Now!"

Joan stopped in her tracks. Her plate of bacon and eggs tilted in one hand. The brown liquid in her mug lolling drunkenly in the other.

"Dulce. Hey, Dulce, it's Fr…" Dottie tried to interrupt.

"That doesn't matter anyway! Who cares when you first met him? I've got him now — he's mine. And I've got something you will never have!"

"Oh, really? Like what?" Dulcie took a step towards her.

Joan matched it and slurped from her mug in a casual catch-me-if-you-can manner. "He bought blue pills for me. Hah! Viagra — for me, see — not for you!"

"Well, I have something that you will never have, Joan Holloway-Potts-Jones. Never in a million years."

"Hah! I doubt that. What could you possibly have that I could never have?"

There was a gap in the silence, as if it too was holding its breath. Dottie and Dee knew what was coming and couldn't believe Dulcie was going to say it out loud.

"His child — his daughter. My daughter, Stella — is Frank's."

Joan dropped the mug, the liquid splashing on the floor.

Behind Dulcie, a quiet voice. "Stella is mine?"

Dulcie spun round, and one foot caught underneath her and down she went.

Frank strode to her side and lifted her into a sitting position.

Dulcie sobbed. "I've been trying to tell you for days, Frank. Stella is yours. You're her father. I only found out after you'd left for Saigon. She was born eight months later. She's our daughter, Frank. Ours."

A wail sliced through the room and Joan dropped like a dead puppet into the middle of the floor. Samuel leapt out of his seat screaming, "You've killed her. I knew you would. I knew you were killing her."

"Someone get a doctor," Prudence murmured as if she could care less.

"I'll get Dr Prince," said Dottie who had risen from the table and was heading for reception.

"Greek in scope," tittered Dee.

Dr Prince galloped into the room and raced to Joan's side. Samuel had managed, with Mike Partridge's help, to turn her onto her back and was crooning over her like a lovesick gorilla.

Prudence's head was on the table, her shoulders shaking.

Dr Prince checked Joan's pulse. "She's alive. Madge, are you there? Madge?"

"Yes, Dennis … er … Doctor, right here."

"Did you call an ambulance?"

"Yes, on its way. Ten minutes I think."

"What's this?" He held up a piece of the broken mug and sniffed it. "It's had coffee in it. Who's is it?"

"Joan was drinking it before she fell," said Dulcie, nursing her own ankle that was swelling like a puffer fish.

"But this is coffee. Joan's allergic to coffee."

"She must've poured it." Samuel pointed accusingly at Dulcie.

"Hardly. She already had it in her hand. I haven't even got mine yet."

"Yes, you did. I saw you."

Everyone started talking at once: those defending Dulcie, those defending Joan.

"Shut up. SHUT UP! All of you," yelled the doctor. "This is not helping. Madge, collect all the broken bits and put them in a bag. If she dies, we'll need to get them tested."

Samuel keened.

The doctor bent to Joan again with his stethoscope on her chest, looked in her eyes and felt her pulse.

"Weak, but there. Lucky. Let's get a pillow or something under her head."

Samuel took off his shirt, exposing his skinny chest under his white vest, and laid it on the floor under Joan's head.

A screech of sirens heralded the ambulance's arrival. Doors banged and suited-up paramedics marched into the room followed by Paul Longley, alerted at last to the emergency.

"What's going on?" he said, bewildered.

"S'cuse us, sir. Clear the way, please." The older and larger of the two ambulance officers pushed Major Longley out of the way.

"Hey, just a minute. I'm the Superintendent here."

"I don't care if you're Winston Churchill mate. This is a medical emergency."

"Yes, but…"

"Not yet, sir. Later if you must, but we're a bit busy. What happened here, doc?"

"Anaphylactic shock brought on by drinking a beverage she's allergic to. Or it could have been a heart attack. Or both, not sure."

"Not sure? You're the doctor in this place, and you're not sure!"

"Yes, but..."

"Out the way then doc, we'll take her." The ambulance officer examined the patient, loaded her onto the gurney and carted her off to the ambulance.

Nobody said a word as Joan was wheeled out of the home.

Then everyone spoke at once.

Frank grabbed the doctor's arm. "Dr Prince, could you take a look at Dulcie's ankle?"

"Oh, goodness, I'd not even noticed. That doesn't look very good, Dulcie. Can you carry her to surgery Frank and I'll bandage it up?"

Frank nodded and bent to lift Dulcie.

"I don't think so. I'm not as light as I used to be."

"No, hmm. I'll get a chair."

The doctor marched off in the direction of the surgery, and Paul Longley, perceiving it to be safe, came into the dining room.

"Who can tell me what happened here?"

Everyone spoke at once and nothing useful was said.

"Stop! Everyone be quiet! I'll come and question you one by one. We'll get to the bottom of this."

Dottie rolled her eyes and Dee giggled. "Best of luck!" She and Dottie went to Dulcie who was still sitting on the cold tiles.

"I'll get piles if I stay here much longer. Can you get me up?"

Dr Prince arrived back with the wheelchair and Frank helped lift Dulcie into it. Together they wheeled her off to the surgery, leaving Dottie and Dee to head out to the lounge to pick up their day's routine, or get in the queue for Major Longley's interrogation.

"What happened?" Dr Prince eyed them in turn.

Frank looked at Dulcie for the explanation; he'd only arrived at the dramatic end and he was still in shock.

Dulcie recounted the saga of the toilet paper, the ruckus outside her room, the morning's revelation and finally, Joan's collapse.

"I'm assuming neither of you tampered with the coffee?" said Dr Prince securing the bandage around Dulcie's ankle with a bandage pin.

"Of course not," said Frank. "I'd only just arrived and as Dulcie said, she hadn't even served herself — still hasn't for that matter — you must be starving."

"I could do with a cup of tea, or something stronger right now. How's my foot, Doctor?"

"You'll live. No tennis for a while though." He chortled, forever the comedian. "You'll need a cane."

"Oh, yes, where is it? I left it in the dining room. Frank, would you, my love?"

Frank got up with a nod and left the surgery.

"So what's really going on?"

"Oh dear! Joan was going on about the blue pills making Frank hers. I'd had a rotten night and had taken a sleeping pill, and when she attacked me saying that Frank loved her and not me, that she had something I would never have, I couldn't handle it anymore. I told her that Frank was Stella's father! Then she collapsed."

"And Frank didn't know?"

"No, I hadn't had a chance to tell him. I'd been trying to find the right moment for days and I thought last night would be it. Then it all went crazy!"

"So Frank arrived just as you said it! Oh dear, poor Frank?"

"Yes, exactly. Poor Frank. I have some explaining to do, I think."

"Well, you'll have at least twenty-four hours of peace to do it. Joan won't be out of the hospital until tomorrow at the very earliest.

But Dulcie … oh hello Frank, well done …" Frank passed a cup of tea and the cane to Dulcie and sat beside her. "Dulcie … and you Frank, I think it's time to tell the major what's been going on. Don't you?" He nodded and walked to a cupboard, grabbed a handful of painkillers, and passed them to Dulcie. "Take a couple of these in case that ankle gets too painful and keep it elevated as much as you can."

He went to the door, and it was obvious they'd been dismissed. Dulcie took a swig of her tea and put the mug on the doctor's desk. Frank took her arm to help her out of the chair.

"I'll come and support you if you wish. It might also be the time to tell him about … you know … your history and your engagement. He might even have some ideas about bedroom re-organization — he's not going to want to lose you. You're too valuable to him, fee wise!" Dr Prince smiled, shook Frank's hand and patted Dulcie on the back.

"Just let me know if you want my input. In the meantime, best of luck."

Frank and Dulcie made their way to the lounge. Dulcie chuckled. "Well, you did say we could use 24 hours of Joan-free time. Looks like we've got it!" She looked up at Frank. His expression was closed.

"Frank? Did you hear what I said? We've got some peace at last."

"Oh yes, darling. Sorry. I was miles away. Yes, of course. Good isn't it? Excellent."

Dulcie squinted up at him. She'd lost her glasses.

***

Major Longley had finished his interrogations in the dining room, and the residents had gone their separate ways.

Dottie and Dierdre were parked in their chairs inside the lounge as it was raining outside; a light drizzle, cooling and pleasant as so often occurs during tropical autumns … winters, springs and summers for that matter.

"The major wants to see you two. Oh, Dulce. Here — your specs — they were on the floor — lucky they didn't get trampled in the panic!" Dottie scratched her nose with a knitting needle.

"Thanks, Dot. You're a star! What did you tell him?"

"Only what happened this morning, nothing else. That's for you, we thought."

Dee was nodding to her music. Dottie rolled her eyes.

Frank took Dulcie's arm and grinned at Dottie. "Right, time to pay the piper huh! If we're not back by lunchtime, send out a search party!"

Dulcie led Frank to Major Longley's office. She hadn't been there very often but she knew the way. She knocked.

"Enter!"

Frank opened the door and poked his nose inside. "You wanted to see us, Major?"

"Ah, Chambers. Sorry, Mr Chambers. Come on in." Paul Longley rose from his chair and extended his hand. "Bit of a rum morning, eh? Want to tell me your side of things? Mrs Dooley?"

"Yes, of course." Dulcie sat in one of the two chairs in front of the major's desk, but Frank stayed standing behind her. He was standing at attention as if in a senior officer's presence.

"Do sit down, Mr Chambers. Sergeant wasn't it, in the war? Vietnam?"

"Yes, sir … er … Mr Longley … goodness, old habits die hard, don't they?"

"You probably feel like you're in trouble, eh? Up on a charge, right? Ha! Ha!" He chortled, lit a cigar. "Hope you don't mind, nasty habit!"

Dulcie looked sideways at Frank as he sat in the chair next to her and raised an eyebrow.

"So, what's been going on? I gather this morning's episode is not an isolated incident. Want to fill me in?"

An hour later they escaped.

Major Longley had shown remarkable reserve during the telling, only bursting out laughing a couple of times; at inappropriate moments, Dulcie thought. The itching powder thing had really tickled him. The final revelation left him gawping, but once he'd realised its significance he could see their point in wanting to be married. He didn't know where he would put them, but as Dr Prince had intimated, he didn't want to lose them. He would find a way. Leave it with him, and congratulations to boot!

They left. Dulcie limped with the support of her cane and Frank walked slowly beside her.

Dulcie was relieved it was over, but a tiny niggle in the back of her mind made her wonder if indeed it was. Joan would be back soon — if she didn't die. What would happen then? And why had she been drinking coffee?

Chapter 14

'Make tea, not war.'
Monty Python

The only person unhappy about Joan's absence was Samuel, and he had taken to his bed. This left Prudence alone for her meals until Mike took pity on her and invited her to his table. Prudence accepted with a sigh of inevitability; she knew Samuel would never be hers so she might as well spread her favours. At least Joan was out of the way; one should be thankful for small mercies.

Lunchtime in the home was peaceful, almost desolate, such was the excitement generated by the feud and the subsequent anticlimax now one of the participants had nearly died. Conversations at the tables focused on what would happen next; once the denizen of Rosehill returned.

No one was asking the obvious question. Had Joan had a heart attack after the revelation of Frank's paternity, or had she suffered an allergic reaction to the coffee? Or both? They didn't really care but they wanted the spice back in their lives.

They were about to get it.

Major Paul Longley, sideburns brushed to a sparkle, khaki shorts pressed to a paper fold, entered the dining room with a clipboard under his arm. He coughed.

Heads rose from white plates still dimpled with the debris of another carbon-copy meal, and eyes peered at the superintendent through misty spectacles.

Frank took Dulcie's hand. Dottie laid down her knitting and kicked Dee under the table.

"What? What now?"

Dottie nodded at the bespectacled major and Dee twisted in her seat to get a better view.

"Huck…hum!" Longley tapped his clipboard with his pen.

"I am sure you are all wondering how Mrs Holloway-Potts-Jones is doing. You'll be pleased to know that she is recovering well and will be home tomorrow afternoon."

A mixed groan rose from the assembly. The major cleared his throat again.

"It appears her collapse was caused by a mild myocardial infarction — heart attack to you — brought on by stress and the inadvisable ingestion of coffee. Further investigations are being carried out regarding the coffee mix-up and the kitchen staff are being interrogated."

Dulcie looked at Frank; his expression was unreadable. He squeezed her hand under the table and she frowned slightly.

The major continued. "For the moment I would like for you all to stay close by in case we need to have another chat with you. Thank you." He smacked his thigh with the clipboard, winced and marched out.

The Teapots returned to their unfinished meals, Dottie chuckled. "What does he think we're going to do, escape to Hawaii?"

Dulcie leaned towards Frank.

"I haven't shown you the tennis court yet, Frank. Let's take a little walk, or a little limp in my case." She rose from the table, grabbed her cane and extended her arm for Frank's support. She smiled at Dottie and Dierdre. "Anon, Teapots, anon!"

They laughed. Dottie inscribed an 'x' with her knitting needle and Dee did her three-time-baton swish.

"Where are we going?"

"Just away from here. We need to have a talk. About Stella as much as anything else."

"It's all right, my darling. It's absolutely marvellous. Was that the photo you tried to show me at the beach? How old is she now?"

Dulcie nodded. "She's 48! And she doesn't know anything. I wanted to tell you about her — about her birth. She's very dark like you. So much like you, but it never occurred to her that she wasn't Bob's. I don't think. Now I'm not sure how to handle it. But handle it we will. She'll be coming for a visit in a few days. We can tell her then."

"We might be getting married then, or would you rather delay it until you've told her. What about telling her on Saturday and getting married the next day? Can they do it that quick?"

"Yes, I think they can. We'll have to announce it though, officially. I think Major Longley can do the service. He's got one of those celebrant certificates on his wall. Did you see it?"

Frank frowned. "No, I didn't, but that would be good. Easier than getting someone else in, and I don't really want to delay it any more. We've already waited fifty years."

They arrived at the tiny tennis court. They'd passed the pool on the way and Dulcie had chuckled. Frank had shaken his head as if nothing further needed to be said about that almost disastrous incident. There were tables positioned to one side of the court as if there would be an audience to the annual Rosehill Wimbledon; chairs were propped up against them and Dulcie chose one in the shade.

"There's something else, Frank. Something I'm confused about." Frank set the two chairs on their feet and they sat down.

"What's that, my darling?" Frank took her hand.

"Do you know anything about the coffee? Why Joan was drinking coffee?"

"Good lord, no! Of course not! Why would you suggest such a thing? I'd only just arrived in the dining room. How would I know anything about it?" Frank got up. "Why would you think that, Dulcie." He stopped. "What do you know about it?"

"Nothing, Frank, nothing. I hadn't long been there myself — it just seemed, well, a bit of a coincidence that we'd said we'd like to have 24 hours peace and quiet, and suddenly we've got it … I thought … perhaps. No, of course not, silly me. Forget I even mentioned it."

But Frank was in a lather. "How could you think I would do something like that, Dulcie? How could you? You know me better than that surely? Joan might be a pain in the backside but I wouldn't try to harm her. Unlike what she's been doing to you, I might add! I've been trying to placate her, put her off kindly — anyway, I didn't know she was allergic to coffee."

"Oh, didn't you? I thought you did. I thought everyone knew. But, of course, I don't think you'd do something like that. But, I haven't seen you for nearly fifty years. Many things have changed. Oh dear, I have messed things up haven't I? Please — forget I even mentioned it."

Frank turned to her, his face a mask. She really didn't know this man anymore; she had no idea what he was capable of, and suddenly she was frightened.

Then he smiled, walked to her, took her hands and pulled her to her feet. "No, darling, of course. We both need to get to know each other again. We're not strangers, but in a way we are. So much has happened over the years. But we have a lifetime to catch up, to find out about those things, whatever they may be. Nothing to worry about — nothing at all."

He took her in his arms and held her tight, but her heart pitter-pattered like fat raindrops on an iron roof. She put her fears to one side and let herself be hugged by this stranger she'd never stopped loving.

***

Peace and calm permeated the Home over the next thirty-six hours. Anticipation could be heard in titters of conversation held behind newspapers and in quiet corners. Samuel stayed in his room. Prudence looked almost chipper, her white pageboy hair cut bouncing in time with Mike's conversation. Her glasses swung around her neck and bounced on her chest as she laughed at his jokes. Cards and mahjong, dominoes and drafts click-clacked in harmony with the mood. Meals brought no surprises apart from an unusual dinner of vegetable lasagne that was laced with rosemary instead of garlic, and served with rice instead of soggy lettuce. Residents picked rice from their false teeth with the end pieces of their spectacles and left the maggoty-grains on their plates.

Frank and Dulcie joined Dottie and Dierdre for dinner then breakfast, lunch and dinner the following day without interruptions. Dee told Frank of her musical career, her concert appearances and her wish to play for them at their wedding. Dottie told Frank about her grandchildren, in particular the baby soon to be swaddled in layers of freshly-knitted yellow cardigans. They would be coming to the wedding, of that they could be sure. Frank told them of his career in Townsville, mindful not to talk too much about Beryl and Michael, but expounding on his successes with idle students whose artistic gifts had been hard to develop.

Dulcie had not forgotten Frank's response to her question about the coffee and she couldn't help but think that his reaction had been odd. She was unsure if she should just let it drop, but having no idea how to discover the truth she was left with no choice. Something was off but she knew not what. Frank appeared unaware of her quandary, and had taken her for little walks in the garden being careful not to work her sprained ankle too hard; the doctor had said some exercise was good but not to overdo it.

And then it was over. Joan was back. Major Longley appeared with her in tow the following lunchtime.

"Attention please, all those with ears to hear." Knives and forks were placed quietly on plates and the requested ears were turned towards the arrivals.

"Wonderful news! We have our dear Joan back!" He clapped his hands enthusiastically encouraging similar behaviour, and a brief medley broke out.

Joan offered a timid smile but avoided looking at Frank and Dulcie. Longley steered her to her table which was currently vacant, Prudence having decamped to Mike's, Samuel still in his room.

"Do I have to sit here on my own? Where is everyone?" Joan, the black Mary Quant firm on her head, looked around the room with a pained expression. Prudence lowered her eyes and Mike patted her hand. "Frank, would you and Dulcie join me?"

Dulcie's eyebrows shot to the ceiling. She got slowly to her feet and turned to face Joan. Frank stood beside her and took her arm.

"That's the spirit," crowed Longley. "The spirit of friendship Rosehill is so famous for. Excellent. That's what I want to see from now on. No more of those silly pranks. You're not children you know, so there's no need to behave like them. We only have happy, friendly residents at Rosehill."

Frank and Dulcie took their seats at Joan's table not daring to look at her. Her black hair was smoothly lacquered, ensuring the failure of any attempt to escape its position.

"Wonderful, jolly good. That's what we want — harmony!" Major Longley turned on his heel, slapped his thigh with his hand and strode out.

"He's a goose, isn't he?" Dee tittered to Dottie.

"An eejit darlin', that's what he is. We'll see how this goes. It won't be what he thinks, and that's for sure and definite."

"Can we get you some lunch, Joan?" said Frank.

"No, no, Frank, thank you. You get some for Dulcie if you haven't had some already. I can help myself."

Frank raised his eyebrows at Dulcie, and she nodded. "That'd be nice, Frank. Thank you."

Frank followed two steps behind Joan as she made her way to the servery. She helped herself to the obligatory meat and salad and turned, plate piled high, to face Frank.

"This is not over, Frank," she hissed. "Not by a long chalk. I know what you did and you will not get away with it. You'll pay. You wait and see."

She smiled brightly and made her way back to the table.

Frank returned with two plates full of the usual lunchtime mess and sat heavily in his chair. He looked hard at Dulcie who peered questioningly at him. He had gone quite pale. He gave a microscopic shake of his head. His mouth was pinched and hard and he'd lost his appetite.

"I'm actually not very hungry today. I'm going to go to my room. Dulcie?"

"Oh, yes. No. I'm not hungry either. I'll come with you. Goodbye, Joan. Glad you're feeling better. See you later." Dulcie rose to meet Frank who took her arm. She picked up her cane from the other table and limped out of the dining room, nodding at Dottie and Dee as they passed.

"Bye, bye, you two lovebirds. See you at dinner!" Joan called gaily, tucking into her food as if someone would steal it.

"What was that about? She's gone nuts again, hasn't she?" Dulcie whispered as they crossed the lounge.

"Sit, Dulcie. Sit a second." Dulcie sat on the highest chair she could find; it wasn't easy getting out of the low ones with only one working lever.

"What?"

"She threatened me. She said, 'this is not over. I know what you did.' She hasn't changed — she just got sneakier."

"What does she mean, 'she knows what you did.' What does she think you did? Frank?"

"I don't know, but I'm going to the kitchen to ask my own questions. Something's not right here. You stay put, darling. I won't be long."

Frank made his way around the side of the building. He went into the kitchen by the back door.

Dulcie looked at her hands, considered a knuckle nibble, but decided against it. She needed to know what was being said in the kitchen; she needed to eavesdrop. She pulled herself up leaning on her cane, and took one careful step after the other. Wretched ankle, she cussed to herself.

She knew the back entrance to the kitchen well. Many were the times she'd helped lay tables for special occasions, to-ing and fro-ing through the dining room swing doors. She hid behind the back door and listened.

"Sarah, I didn't ask you to do anything to the coffee urn. I only asked you how much it held and how the liquid was served. Did you do something to it?"

"No, I didn't do nothing, Mr Chambers, I promise. But the major thinks I did, and that I did it on purpose 'cause I like you and Mrs Dooley, and I don't like seeing what the hyena's been doing to youse. I heard all about it, ya see."

"What does he think you did?"

"He thinks I let the tea urn empty and put the tea sign on the coffee one. But everyone else would have noticed if I'd done that, wouldn't they? It don't make no sense." Sarah started crying.

Frank patted her shoulder and passed her his handkerchief. "Here, have a blow, Sarah. How can this have happened then?"

"I dunno, Mr Chambers. I really don't know."

Dulcie left her hiding place and limped back to the lounge. Frank would be out of the kitchen soon. She needed to beat him back. She didn't make it.

"Where've you been Dulcie?"

"Um … nowhere. La-ta?"

"Where?"

"La-ta. It's what we call the lav."

"But Dulcie the lav's over there by the dining room. Not by the kitchen door." Frank searched her eyes. "Were you listening?"

Dulcie pattered towards the lift and banged on the button. "I'm going up for a nap now, Frank."

"Hey, Dulcie, stop. What do you think's going on here?"

"I don't know, Frank. Do you?"

"Yes, I think I do. But I'm not sure."

"Not sure, eh, Frank? Not sure? You ask Sarah about coffee urns and then Joan collapses with an allergy attack. Bit of a coincidence, don't you think? For someone who doesn't know, you sure seem to know a lot." She was furious. She'd never had a real argument with Frank, but this certainly felt like one.

The lift arrived and she hurried in, hitting the button on the inside and letting the door shut on Frank's astonished face. She reached her room and locked the door behind her.

She slumped into her comfy chair and buried her head in her hands. Frank had talked to Sarah about the coffee urn. Sarah had said she'd done nothing. Had Frank switched the signs before he'd come in that morning? It was the only answer. It had to have been him. And Joan nearly died.

Dulcie didn't know what to do. Should she go to Major Longley and tell him of her suspicions? Should she keep quiet and see what happened? She should definitely keep out of Joan's way that was for sure. And Frank's for that matter, until she'd worked out what to do. She couldn't believe the man she loved could have done something like this, but all the evidence pointed that way.

She lay on her bed looking up at the ceiling — was inspiration to be found up there? She turned onto her side and closed her eyes. Maybe the answer would come in a dream.

Chapter 15

'Dad was at his desk when I opened the door, doing what all British people do when they're freaked out: drinking tea.'
Rachel Hawkins, Demonglass

Frank stared bewildered as Dulcie disappeared into the lift. Could she really believe he would try and kill Joan? Great God, she actually did. But if he hadn't, who had? Perhaps a nap would do him good. Get some inspiration from the shredded wallpaper.

"Frank. Mr Chambers?" Paul Longley was striding towards him from the kitchen. "Could I have a word, please?"

"Certainly. Here?"

"No, in my office I think. Safer. Walls have ears."

Frank followed him down the back corridor to his office and closed the door. He sat in the chair Dulcie had occupied a couple of days before and it made him feel sad. He hoped he wasn't losing the woman he loved because of a dreadful misunderstanding.

"Frank. This is a frightful business isn't it? Poor Joan. But I think we've uncovered the culprit. Young Sarah … in the kitchen. She put coffee in the tea urn, we think … that's what caused the problem. I've had to fire her I'm afraid, can't have that sort of thing happening here at Rosehill. Get us a frightful reputation, what!"

"To say nothing of having to admit that a resident was almost killed in house by a member of staff, and losing the income she represents. Yes, I can see that would be awkward."

"Ah, yes! I can tell you understand completely!" Frank couldn't believe his ears. This joker thought he had a comrade in arms because they were both of a military background.

"So here's the rub. Sarah must go, she's as much as admitted that someone put the idea in her head, and that she hates Joan Holloway-Potts-Jones."

"Did she say who put the idea in her head?"

"No, she's keeping very quiet about it. Can't get that out of her. So she'll go at the end of the week. Won't be difficult to replace her. Girls like her are two-a-penny. So with luck we should be back on an even keel in time for your wedding!" He polished his nails on his lapel.

"I see," said Frank, not sure where the conversation was heading.

"So. What I'd like to do is to follow a ghastly episode with a happy one. Your wedding! One week from Sunday would be perfect. That gives you and Dulcie ten days to get yourselves organised, invite your families and guests. Sort out your honeymoon, etcetera. Ha! Ha! And be ready for the day. What do you think? Good idea, what?"

"Er … sounds fine to me but I'll need to check with Dulcie. I know her daughter … um … our daughter is due at the weekend, so perhaps Dulcie can discuss it with her. Can I get back to you?" Frank tried to imagine all the objections Dulcie might have, but apart from the obvious one — was her fiancé a homicidal maniac — he couldn't think of any.

"Yes, fine. No problem. Dr Prince and I thought we could do a little bedroom shuffling, particularly now yours has had the wallpaper ripped — goodness what a thing — we can work it so you and the beautiful soon-to-be Mrs Chambers, can have a double room — married quarters, what — organised for you before you get back from your honeymoon. How would that be? Anyway, I'd like to announce it tomorrow at lunch if that works for you. Pop by in the morning and let me know. Ok? Good! Excellent! Splendid!" The major rose and appeared to be about to salute. Frank rose accordingly but kept his hand in his pocket. Longley extended his palm. Frank accepted it in time-honoured fashion, and bade him good day.

Outside the lift Frank considered his options. He took the stairs. He knocked quietly on Dulcie's door. No reply. He knocked again, a little firmer this time. He heard a rustle from inside.

"Who is it?"

"It's me. Can I come in — please?" He had to come clean; it was the only way. He couldn't start a marriage with lies. She had to know — everything.

The door opened a crack and he could see she'd been crying.

"I'm not feeling very well, Frank. Can it wait?"

"Not really, Dulcie. It's pretty important."

"It's always important with you, isn't it? Always more important than what I have to say! Oh, come in then." She left him to open the door fully, and flounced off back to the bed. He'd never seen her flounce before, it was actually quite charming, but then he thought everything about this woman was charming. Always had been and, he suspected, always would be.

"Sit, Dulcie, please."

"I am sitting!"

"Oh, so you are. I am guessing that you heard my conversation with Sarah but I have to tell you the rest of it."

"Might be a good start."

"Dulcie, please, bear with me. It's not what you're thinking."

"Oh really! And you know what I'm thinking now do you, Frank Chambers?"

"Well, I always used to know what you were thinking, and I've got a pretty good idea."

"All right then. You're on. Stage is yours. I'm listening."

"Ok. Well. I wanted to know if the urns could pour mulled wine or champagne. So I asked Sarah if the champagne would stay cold if it sat in the urns for a long time, or if mulled wine would be better, being as it's cooler now, you see. I had a plan to announce our engagement at breakfast and surprise everyone by having champagne come out of the urns instead of tea. It was quite innocent — and had nothing to do with coffee."

Dulcie stared at Frank. Then she shook her head, trying to choose between a scowl or a smile.

"Why didn't you tell me before — you're a ninny sometimes, Frank, you really are."

"It was supposed to be a surprise."

"Turned into a bigger surprise than you imagined I'd say. Oh dear, I'm sorry I doubted you, Frank. You should be furious with me."

"I can understand it, I think. But here's a funny thing that did happen just after I'd been talking to Sarah, who by the way, does not deserve to be fired and I will do everything I can to get her reinstated. But Longley has got it in for her because he can't think of any other solution. But here's the thing, when I came out of the kitchen that day I nearly knocked Prudence flying. I think she'd been listening at the door."

***

In a retirement home, one day is pretty much like another. The residents often have little events to look forward to: internet lessons on Thursdays for those with laptops, usually well attended, ping-pong lessons on Tuesdays from 10 to 11, movies on Friday evenings, and the odd excursion to the beach or the city. But the most exciting always was a birthday. They were more than just a celebration of another year survived; they were landmarks, achievements, successes!

Then, there were the rarest of occasions, ones that would engender excitement, jealousy, rummaging in wardrobes for outfits, trips to Cairns in taxis, hair-dos and manicures; all instigated by an announcement. This particular Thursday, after breakfast and before the laptop lesson, came such an announcement; one that put them all into a tizzy.

Major Longley, armed with whip and clipboard, barrelled into the lounge resplendent in fez and red, white and blue sarong for reasons best known to himself. He winced when he cracked his whip on his thigh, the sarong being made of thinner material than his normal khaki shorts. Undaunted by the pain, he tapped the whip on the clipboard and after clearing his throat launched into a speech as though he were the Master of Ceremonies in a circus.

"Ladies and gentlemen! Your attention please." Tap! Tap! "Many of you, well probably all of you in fact, know of the enduring love affair between our very own Dulcie Dooley and her long lost love, Frank Chambers, who met again by the stars' light here at our wonderful Rosehill."

"Get on with it." Mike Partridge sniggered from the back of the room.

"Ah yes, quite right! Well, where was I? Right. So, we are to have a wedding! Yes, settle down now, oh…"

"We're all quite settled, just tell us when and where!" Mike was keen to get to his laptop lesson with Prudence.

"Right, yes. When? Sunday week. Where? Here of course, where else?" He cheered. "Hurrah, hurrah."

Applause skittered around the room. "Can we get our grand-kids up?" said Mrs Stillson.

"Can we drink ourselves silly at your expense?" said Mr Stilwell, of one of the double rooms on the upper floor.

"Yes, yes, all of that. It will be our pleasure to treat you all to a glass of champagne."

"Or five. Miserly old git," said Dave, happily hidden by Mike Partridge and Prudence.

"Right, yes, whatever you want. So let's have a big hand for Frank Chambers and Dulcie Dooley." He broke into strains of Cliff Richard's *Congratulations* — except he was singing on his own.

"Where are Frank and Dulcie?"

"I think they escaped just before you started, Major. Last seen heading for Frank's bedroom I'd say. Something to celebrate now, eh?" Dottie was glad that Dulcie and Frank hadn't been there to hear the major's embarrassing warble.

"Ah yes, of course. We can relax our special rules for them, I think. Good. Well, that'll be all then. Two o'clock Sunday next. All in your best outfits, obviously. Good. Bye for now." He strutted off slapping his whip against the clipboard again.

"Buffoon!" said Dierdre. "Did they really head for the bedroom, I thought they'd gone down the garden."

"I don't know Deeds, but if I'd been them I'd have made my escape anywhere handy. I'm guessing the bedroom. They've certainly got lots of time to make up for!"

Joan had been sitting at the back of the room, hidden by a large potted palm. Her hands were clenching into fists and she was tapping them against her thighs in her familiar school-born rhythm. Her face, under the black Mary Quant, was purple.

"I can't let this happen," she muttered, "they can't be allowed to win. They cannot win." She rose from the chair and stalked from the room. No one noticed her, Samuel was still abed.

Joan slinked out of the lounge. Residents were thronging as if a great excitement was upon them, talking in riddles about their outfits for the wedding, everyone talking to everyone, and no one listening. She took the lift up to her room and closed the door behind her. Some prepared items were ranged on her bedside table where she'd inspected them every night since her plan had commenced. She popped a little packet into her pocket; that would do the job.

She made her way to Frank's room, and taking his key from her pocket, she turned it in the lock. She knew they were in there, she could hear them laughing; laughing at her. She took the small gaffer-taped packet of one-dollar coins, and squeezed them into the crack of the door jam. They stuck tight. There'd be no getting out of that room. Oh no! They wanted a room to themselves. They've got one now, forever.

She headed downstairs and took the back corridor to the external kitchen entrance. She peeked inside and saw Sarah cleaning the stove getting it ready for the lunchtime preparation; she wasn't leaving until Friday. It was Thursday. Chips were the order of the day. The gas was on and the oil was heating up.

She sauntered in.

"Hello Sarah," she said, her voice low and calm.

Sarah looked up in alarm. No one was allowed in the kitchen, it was a staff only area.

"Mrs. Holloway-Potts-Jones? You're not supposed to be in here."

"And you're not supposed to be poisoning residents, are you, Sarah?"

Sarah's heart leapt. "I don't know what you are talking about Mrs. Holloway-Potts-Jones. Honestly I don't. No one poisoned anyone. And you're not supposed to be in here. Please leave now!"

"Oh, very commanding Sarah. Did you command Frank Chambers in the same way? Did you seduce him so he would do what you wanted or was it the other way round? Did he put his little penis in your hand and get you to pull it for a bit and then ask you to poison the coffee so I would die? Did he? Did you?" Joan advanced on Sarah picking up the gas lighter on her way.

"Mrs Holloway-Potts-Jones, I can't imagine where you'd get such an idea. That's an outrageous, disgusting suggestion. Please leave now!" Sarah backed away colliding with the fridge full of afternoon cakes.

Joan lit a gas burner and turned it up high.

"You can't do that. They need to have pots on top of them; they can't just burn. We'll run out of gas. You'll get no lunch."

"I don't care if I never have one of your stinking lunches ever again. It deserves to go up in flames, just like you."

Joan turned the chip fryer up. The fat began to bubble.

"Bubble, bubble, toil and trouble, Sarah. That's what you've been doing isn't it? Making trouble."

Sarah screamed. Joan put the gas lighter into the fat and it exploded.

"Look at your face, Sarah. Terrified of fire. When you're old like me you're not frightened of anything except being alone. Let this ridiculous place burn down. It's insured. Let them all burn. We'll all go to hell at the same time and who will care? No one. Only Major Ludicrous Longley who'll lose his income. Let it burn, let it burn!"

She lit every other burner, threw some dishrags and tea towels on to the flames and roared her manic, hyena laugh into Sarah's horrified face. Then, she fled through the back door.

Sarah raced for the fire extinguisher and pointed it at the fire, but there were several fires, not just one, and she didn't know which one to point it at first. She tried them all but had no luck. The fat was burning and she couldn't get close enough to put it out. She only had two choices: run and save herself, or try to put the fire out and maybe perish in the doing. She'd been fired — what a ridiculous expression she thought. This was what being fired looked like. Being set on fire by a mad woman bent on revenge. She whirled around brandishing the fire extinguisher but the flames had hit the ceiling and were lapping it up like a toddler at the cupcakes. Already a hole in the plaster was forming. Sarah knew enough about fires to know that if it went through the ceiling the whole of the upper level would ignite. The Home was built of dry old timber. It would burn like kindling.

Sarah made a decision. She ran. The back door was open, but the door to the dining room was blocked by flames. She ducked to the sink and grabbed some towels, wet them and made a bundle. The smoke was becoming thicker, the air getting harder to breathe. She took a deep breath and threw the wet towels over her head and charged for the back door. A sudden blast of heat radiated up her leg and ignited her skirt. She ripped it away from her body. Her skin was singed and her underwear was smoking. She doused her body in the wet towels and made another dash for the door.

In the distance a fire engine's siren punctuated the noise of the roaring flames. She heard maybe two or even three, but knew they would be too late for her if she didn't get out. She bent double and ran into the flames; there was no other way. She held her breath and bolted for the door. She could feel the flames licking at her legs, and tried not to scream. The flames were reaching higher and higher and the timbers creaked as they came loose. One beam fell into the middle of the kitchen scattering pots of flaming oil. Sarah crawled as fast as she could through blazing hobs, burning dollops of fat, and charcoaled chips. She reached the door, her clothes smoking, and collapsed with the wet towels still wrapped around her head.

***

Frank and Dulcie had escaped to the garden just before Major Longley entered the lounge. They knew what was about to happen; Frank had been to see him earlier in the day to confirm that all was well, Dulcie was happy, the dates were good and he could make the announcement. They just didn't want to be there when he did. They knew it would be a circus so they lit out before he even entered the lounge.

In the garden they made for the dolphins. Frank had told Dulcie about Joan's seduction techniques and Dulcie had tried not to laugh. It all seemed so unfair. Why couldn't Joan pick on someone who was interested in her? She could never tell apparently, but it was over now and they had some time to themselves. They perched on the same bench they'd sat on the first day Dulcie had taken Frank through the garden.

"It's really been a very long time, hasn't it?" said Frank. "I feel as if we're starting again. Meeting for the first time, full of the excitement of not knowing, and yet knowing, the wonderment of newness that isn't really new, and yet it is." His voice was soft, his eyes searching.

"I know."

Frank laid a long, slender finger on Dulcie's lips and followed it with the softest of kisses. "That's it," he said. "You know. I have always known there would be no-one but you. I wonder why the fates decided to make us wait until now to be together again."

"Better late than never. It's an extraordinary stroke that brought us here. I can't believe how lucky we are and yet, while I'm saying that, a part of me is nervous, as if we're tempting fate. We still don't know what happened to Joan, or what she has planned. She said it isn't over, and I for one, believe her. I just can't imagine what else she can do to try and get you away from me. I don't understand why she can't just accept it?"

"I don't know, my darling. I really don't. She's obsessed, and there is no understanding obsession, there never has been. I've seen children with Obsessive Compulsive Disorder washing their hands a thousand times a day, rubbing them raw to remove unseen germs. I've seen them wiping seats and handles and paint brushes in case someone else's germs are on them. There is no explanation. Joan wants a fifth husband. It's a mark of pride for her. She must know that she can't have a child at her age, so she must want a husband in place of a child. She really should marry Samuel. Then, she could pick him up and carry him around like a six-year-old."

Dulcie started giggling. "Oh, Frank don't, the visual is too much."

The sirens interrupted their laughter.

"What's that?"

"It sounds like the fire alarm." Dulcie stood, picking her cane up from the seat. "Perhaps it's a drill. They do that sometimes, but they usually warn us."

Frank rose and sniffed the air. "It's not a drill. I can smell smoke."

“Gosh, you’re right. I can too now. Do you think there’s a problem? Should we go back?”

“Yes, I think we should.”

They hurried towards the house as fast as Dulcie could limp.

The scene that confronted them was like something from a disaster film. The upper half of Rosehill Retirement Home for Gentlefolk was on fire.

“Oh dear God. It looks like something from *Gone with the Wind.* What should we do, Frank? We can’t go near it but what about the people inside? It’s appalling!”

Frank shook his head. “I’ll head up there, see if I can help. Can you manage on your own, Dulcie?”

“Yes, of course, I’ll get there too, you just run!”

Frank broke into a trot nearing the building just as ambulances screeched to a halt and more fire engines screamed up the driveway. Smoke was visible above the roof and screams of pain and panic filled the air.

Some of the residents were gathered outside the front entrance — the designated gathering point for fire drills. But this was certainly no drill.

Great billows of smoke were pouring from the first floor. The lounge and dining room doors were blazing ovens. Flames leapt and danced out of the second floor windows and the roof creaked.

“Dulcie, that’s my window, look!” Frank reached for Dulcie’s hand as she arrived by his side. The fire spread quickly to its neighbour.

“Let’s keep back, I think there will be a stampede. Not sure how many people this place holds but I’m sure it’s more than this. Can you tell who’s missing?”

Dulcie rubbed her glasses on her skirt and peered at the crowd. “I can’t see the Smithsons, they live in No.14 on the upper floor near Joan’s. Joan’s not there either. The Stillwells are, and Mike and Dave and Dottie and Dee — I should go to them. They’ll be worried about us — but at least they knew we were going to the garden."

Frank scanned the throng, but residents rushing about to check on who had got out in time made it impossible to tell who was who, particularly as he only knew a few of them anyway.

"Look, there's Samuel and Prudence. They look like they're arguing. Can you hear what they're saying?" The crackling flames and the water gushing from the fire hoses made it hard to hear anything.

"No, I can't. Let's get a bit closer."

Samuel and Prudence were screaming at each other.

"I can't believe you did that, Prudence. Why? Why? Do you really hate her that much?" Samuel collapsed onto the grass beside the driveway, rocking his little body to and fro.

Prudence bent over him and stroked his back and hair. "Get off me," he yelled, "I can't believe it. You nearly got her killed. Did you do this too?"

Dulcie and Frank could hear their words now and gawped at each other. Frank put his finger to his lips.

"No, I haven't done this. She has, Sam. She's as mad as a meat axe, she's trying to kill Frank and Dulcie. She thinks they're in his room."

"No! Joan couldn't do that, she just couldn't. She's not like that."

"Oh! Sam! Wise up. She's got you totally fooled. She doesn't care about you. I'm the only one who ever cared about you; you've never ever seen that. I had to get rid of her. Typical of the fucking bitch to survive. I hate that woman."

Frank and Dulcie gasped.

A great crack could be heard as another beam came crashing down. Joan ran screaming from the front door.

"They're going to die in there. I locked them in. They can't get out. You've got to get them out of there. That one — up there — that window!" She shook a fireman's arm and pointed to Frank's room. Tears were streaming down her face; her black wig hanging by only a thread.

"Lady, anyone who was in that room is cactus — way past saving."

Joan keened like a bereaved animal pulling at her wig as if to tear it out by the roots.

"We should tell her we're here Dulcie. She's over the edge."

"You're right, let's go." Dulcie hobbled up the grass with Frank holding her arm. He shouted as loud as he could over the din. "Joan! Joan! We're here!"

Joan swivelled and gawped at Frank and Dulcie. Then she folded like a rag doll onto the grass. A big burly fireman took off one of his gloves, felt her pulse and yelled. "Ambulance — here, now!"

Frank and Dulcie rushed to Joan's side, but she was unconscious. Two paramedics arrived with a gurney, felt her pulse again, looked in her eyes and loaded her onto the stretcher. They trotted to the vehicle and wheeled her in.

Samuel ceased his wailing, and staggered to the ambulance. "Joan! Joan! Please don't die. I love you. Please don't die. Can I go with her?" He looked hopefully at the Ambulance men.

"You her husband?"

"Yes," said Sam. "I'm her husband."

"Hop in then." They closed the door on them both, did a swift three point turn and nee-naw-ed down the hill.

Prudence stared open-mouthed when the ambulance left taking Samuel with it. When she saw Dulcie and Frank staring at her, she cried out and backed away down the lawn, dragging her gamy leg behind her.

Chapter 16

'If you are cold, tea will warm you; If you are too heated, it will cool you; If you are depressed, it will cheer you; If you are exhausted, it will calm you.'
William Gladstone

By dinner time the fire was out. The smoldering wreck of Rosehill Retirement Home left the residents homeless, and the management searching for insurance certificates. One area untouched by the fire was the swimming pool and the tennis court. Several rooms had been saved and a couple were even undamaged by water, but there was no suggestion that anyone could remain in the home that night, or the foreseeable future. No one could access their quarters because of damage to the stairs so ambulances took the residents and staff to Cairns Base Hospital, checked them over, distributed night apparel and other essentials, and then released them to emergency billets.

The Teapots knew they would be herded off soon, but they met at the pool to check in, make sure they were all OK, determined to stay together if possible, and learn what, if anything, anyone knew about how the fire started.

"They found Sarah, you know," Dottie said. "She was unconscious at the back door of the kitchen wrapped in wet towels, poor love. I suppose she's at the Base somewhere. We won't be able to find out what she knows — ever maybe, unless we can find her!"

"You were lucky, you two," said Dee, her headphones hanging

around her neck. "Joan was frantic — out of her mind. Kept saying she'd locked you in your room and you couldn't get out. Yelling that she hadn't meant to kill you, just play a little joke on you. She's barking mad."

Dulcie spoke softly, as if in memoriam. "The only people who never appeared were the Smithsons. But, I think they'd gone away for a few days and Longley had forgotten about it. Of course, it was Prudence you know, all along. We heard her telling Samuel she wanted to get rid of Joan."

"I almost feel sorry for her. She was so in love with Samuel. And then he went off in the ambo, saying he was Joan's husband, going on about how he loved her and always had. What a tangled web, eh? Where's Prudence now, does anyone know?" They shook their heads.

Major Longley hobbled up the pathway. "Come on you four, time to go," he said, rubbing his leg. He'd fallen over a bucket that had rolled out of the burning kitchen, and sliced his knee open. Dr Prince had been chasing around like a headless turkey, treating cuts, bruises and burns, bandaging arms and legs — stitching up Paul Longley had been last on his list. "We've been able to find you a place where you can all be together. There'll be an investigation, obviously, and I don't know whether you've thought about your wedding Frank and Dulcie, but a small postponement might be in order. Unless, of course, you want to get married somewhere else."

"We'll give it some thought, Major," said Frank getting to his feet. "There's a lot to take in just at the moment. How will we know if and when we can come back? How we will get in touch with you?"

"Don't you worry about that, my friend. Madge will be in touch. She'll know where everyone is, and once we've salvaged whatever's possible from the rooms, we'll be bringing it all to you. Soon — hopefully. Oh! By the way, have you seen Prudence? Mike's going crazy looking for her."

"Um — not sure actually, Major. We last saw her with Samuel

on the driveway just before he went off with Joan in the ambo." Frank gave Dulcie a look.

"Oh, right then, she's not amongst the wreckage then. That's a good thing, isn't it! We'll keep looking. Come on you lot, time to get you settled."

He limped off shaking his head and rubbing his sideburns.

"Why didn't you tell him?"

"I don't know, didn't seem right. Anyway she's probably not in the garden anymore, even though I can't begin to imagine where she went."

Frank and the Teapots followed Major Longley to the drive where a seven-seater Toyota Torago was waiting. They clambered in and waved goodbye to the smoldering wreck of Rosehill.

"I hope there'll be a phone where we're going. Stella will be frantic if she's heard about the fire. I must call her as soon as possible." Dulcie massaged her temples.

"Ditto for all of us I imagine. I must get hold of Michael. Dottie what about your tribe? Dee, do you have family somewhere? We've never spoken about it before."

"My lot are far, far away. My sons live in America with their families. I get to see them about once a year, but I'll email them once I can get to a computer." Frank was surprised that Dee was computer savvy. There was still a lot he didn't know about these remarkable women.

The taxi arrived at the Cairns Base Hospital and they were shepherded into the emergency area and promptly separated.

Frank complained immediately. "I'm sorry but this lady is my wife — well, my wife to be, we're engaged and I'm not leaving her side."

"All right mate, keep your hair on. We've had a lot of people telling us they're engaged to be married tonight, so you just stay put and we'll look after you both as soon as we can."

"Nurse, can you tell us if a girl called Sarah Trimble was admitted with burns earlier?"

"No, dear, we can't tell you anything like that, unless you're family, then you'd have to go to the burns unit. Was she in the fire too?"

"Yes, in the kitchen. We think that's where it started."

"Right, well, as I say, we can't divulge that information even if we wanted to. Sorry, dear."

Frank took Dulcie's hand and they sat on the seats provided in the cubicles while Dottie and Dee were sent to other areas.

An eternity later, Dulcie and Frank were released having been checked out and judged fit. Major Longley met them outside the emergency room and put them in a taxi to The Green Ant Hostel, who had offered rooms and apartments for the homeless geriatrics. There were no stairs involved and some rooms even had wheel chair access. It appeared that everyone would be there. Except for Joan, Samuel and Prudence who were nowhere to be found.

Chapter 17

'If this is coffee, please bring me some tea;
but if this is tea, please bring me some coffee.'
Abraham Lincoln

The winter days continued in pleasant warmth, temperatures being a little higher near the ocean than in the hills. The erstwhile residents of Rosehill adapted to their new environment: outings were organised, laptop lessons re-established, a piano was found and Dee regaled her audience with classical and modern pieces — practicing, she insisted, for the wedding, the new date of which had yet to be announced.

Frank and Dulcie concentrated on rekindling their love, and preparing for the meeting with Stella.

Dulcie had phoned her daughter as soon as they were settled at The Green Ant, so named for the centimetre-long, green-bottomed insect that nested in every house and garden in North Queensland.

"Stella, it's Mum."

"Oh! Mum! Are you all right? I've been going frantic. I heard about the fire on the news but they said nothing about survivors, or where everybody was, so I had no idea."

"Yes, darling, we're all fine, well mostly. There are still a few missing, but no one was found in the wreckage so everyone is somewhere. I'm so sorry not to have called you before, but we've only just got sorted out. We're at the Green Ant Hostel on Bunda

Street just behind Cairns Central Shopping Centre. Are you coming up? I've got something important to tell you."

"I was going to come up next weekend. What is it, can't you tell me on the phone?" Stella was accustomed to her mother's important things — they rarely were.

"No, darling, this is something I must share with you face to face. It is really important."

"Ok, then. Bart and I can come up on Saturday around midday. We'll take you out for lunch, how about that? Bet you could do with some decent food. Glad you're OK ! See you then. Bye for now, love you!"

Dulcie nodded at Frank. "Saturday midday, lunch somewhere. Hope I don't make a fool of myself. I'm bound to get weepy!"

"I'll be there to support you, my love — and I'll probably get weepy too!" They hugged and went back to their books.

Saturday arrived and Dulcie was in a tizzy! She couldn't make up her mind what to wear even though she knew that clothing was going to be the least important thing on the agenda. A green skirt and top — she'd been shopping at Cairns Central — a currycomb through her hair, a dash of powder on her cheeks, a swipe of lippy and she was set.

They had been allocated a twin room at The Green Ant, and they'd moved the beds together so they could at least hold hands across the divide. Frank's little blue pills had gone up in smoke, and Dr Prince had not been in evidence since the night of the fire. Frank hadn't wanted to bother him with unimportant matters like his sex life. They did without; there was no urgency. They were together again; that was precious gift enough.

At midday, Dulcie was huffing and puffing, scurrying around, driving Frank mad.

"Just sit for a minute, Dulcie, she'll be here when she's here."

"Easy for you to say. I'm just about to present her with a father she never knew she had, as opposed to the one she thought she had, without warning. I'm fully expecting her to storm out of the room and never speak to me again. She can be very volatile you know."

"Do you actually need to tell her? Why don't you come at it from the back entrance…"

The phone in the room rang.

"Yes!"

"Hi Mum, it's us. We're in the courtyard."

Dulcie flushed to her roots. "Ok, darling, on our way!"

"On **our** way…?"

Dulcie cut her off. "Here we go, hell or high water… "

"Darling, you don't need to steam in with that information. Just tell her we're getting married. It'll flow on from there." Frank grabbed her hand, pulling her back from the door. "It'll be all right!"

But Frank was taken aback. It was like looking in a mirror fifty years ago.

"See what I mean?" Dulcie giggled; a nervous giggle that rippled out of her throat as she rushed to her daughter's side and embraced her.

Frank stared. Stella was the spitting image of himself as a youth, except she was pretty and a girl. Her eyes were like his, deep brown molten pools. He could hardly breathe.

"And this is…?" Stella let her mother go and stared at Frank. Her brows knit and she cocked her head to one side.

"This is Frank. Frank Chambers, darling. And we have some news." She smiled, giggled again and brought Frank closer to Stella.

"Hello. How do you do … Frank." Stella stretched her hand out towards Frank, her fingers trembling only slightly.

Frank shook her hand. He didn't want to let it go. He thought he'd come to terms with having a daughter, but this was another matter altogether.

"And the news is…?" Stella refocused on her mother, aware that she'd been stunned by the handsome, elderly man in front of her.

"What about we save it for lunch? Sit down somewhere nice so we can have a chat." Frank knew if Dulcie blurted it out there and then, she would collapse in tears and God only knew how Stella would react. Better to be sitting down; not so far to fall.

"Yes, good idea, Frank. Good, let's go. Bart, where's the car? Oh yes, on the street. Right, let's go then — to Mondo's. It's on the water. Nice, there."

Dulcie and Frank glanced at each other and clasped hands. "Do you think she guessed?" Dulcie whispered.

"She seemed surprised for sure. We'll find out I think … very soon."

Mondo's was a well-known and well-frequented restaurant attached to the Hilton Hotel. It was accessed both through the Hotel, Cairns' premium 5-star hotel, as well as from the road. One usually had to book, especially for a party of four. But they were in luck and were shown immediately to a table situated right next to Trinity Inlet. A cool breeze blew making it almost necessary for a cardigan. But Dulcie was in so much of a fluster that feeling chilly was the last of her concerns. They took their seats and examined the menus.

Stella kept peeking over the top of her menu at Frank, and he worked really hard not to notice. They ordered at the servery and Frank dealt with the bill, requesting cold water and a bottle of Pinot Grigio to go with their fish.

When they'd finished their barramundi and chips, Stella took the lead. "So. What's the news?"

Frank nodded at Dulcie, who nodded back. She didn't think she could speak.

"Stella, Bart. I have asked Dulcie to be my wife." He rushed on, leaving no time for comment. "We were going to married up at Rosehill but then it burned down and now we don't know whe…" he stopped. Stella's hand had popped up like a school child.

"And you've know about this how long?"

"About fif … a few days. We've only just met…"

"Again," they said together.

"Whoa! Wait a minute. You've only just met AGAIN? Please explain — the again part!" Stella sounded a little angry but more perplexed.

Frank took Dulcie's hand and laid it on the table so Stella could see the old engagement ring on her little finger. It had survived the fire and Dulcie hadn't taken it off since. The new one sat on her third finger, because she couldn't get the old one on her third finger off her left hand, her fingers being too fat these days. It matched the original in everything except for size.

"We met fifty years ago, Stella — in Brisbane. We were at University together and we were sweethearts before I was called up for active duty in Vietnam. We were going to get married, but we lost each other. And then, we just met again by chance at Rosehill a couple of weeks ago — I can't believe it's only been a couple of weeks —and now we want to be together, forever." Frank looked into his daughter's eyes and saw bewilderment.

"Anything else I should know?" Stella's brittle tone showed her anger; as if she knew what was coming.

Dulcie sat up straight, looked at her daughter and took a deep breath. "Frank is your father, darling."

Stella shot to her feet, knocking the chair over, and stormed off towards the water. Bart got up to follow her but Frank stopped him. "Leave her, Bart. Give her a minute."

"A minute? She'll need a fucking lifetime after this!" Bart took off after Stella and took her in his arms. She shook him off, shouted something at him and pounded on towards the Pier, a kilometre or so in the distance.

Bart returned to the table. "Why didn't you tell her, Dulcie? She's always wondered why she didn't look like Bob, or you for that matter. You should have told her!"

"There was never a good time, and I thought Frank had been killed in Vietnam. I didn't see the point. It would have raked up very painful memories for no purpose."

"No purpose? You must be kidding. Look at him. Look at Frank. Now look at Stella. They're peas in a pod. Knowing about him would've given her so many answers. Answers she never got thinking Bob was her dad. Dear God, how could you?"

Dulcie began to cry. She never thought they would react like this. She thought, perhaps misguidedly, that Stella would be happy. After all Bob had been dead for seven years.

Frank put his arm around her shoulder while she sobbed. Bart took off after Stella.

"What should we do? Should we just stay and wait for them to come back? I wanted this to be such a happy day."

"Maybe we should just leave and get a cab back to The Green Ant."

"I can't leave it like this, Frank. What if she's OK after a cry and a think? She always was one to react fast and furious — must be her Italian blood!" She giggled between the tears, and Frank hugged her.

"They're coming back, look." Dulcie peered over Frank's shoulder and could see her daughter striding back, her face a thundercloud.

"She doesn't look happy!"

"I don't know what to say to you, Mum. We're going home now. Nice to meet you F… Frank. Best of luck with the wedding!" She picked up her handbag, took Bart's arm and departed.

that Sarah Trimble is fine, and coming back to Rosehill when it opens again, not burned too badly fortunately, and also…"

"That's four things!" The gaggle of Rosehillians crowed in unison.

"All right, all right. I'm just excited, that's all. Yes, the last thing is that we found Prudence, and she's fine and will be back with us soon."

"So you never found out who set the fire then. Or who tried to kill Joan. What've you been doing, Longley? Filling in Insurance forms?"

A communal chortle rocked through the group.

"Ha! Ha! Oh yes, all of that. Investigations still under way. Good, right that's it then." And he made to leave.

"When's the bloody wedding then?" Potted palm in full throttle.

"Oh, yes, good point! Next weekend. Er … Saturday. Here. 14.00 hours. Right. Bye for now!" and off he trotted.

"Why does he bother with a clipboard if he never reads what's on it? He's an idiot, isn't he?" Dee chuckled.

"So who's getting married then? Apart from you two," said Dottie.

"No idea. And if they found Prudence, where is she?" said Frank.

"Do you think Longley had a plant?" Dulcie said.

"A plant? Whoever it was, was hidden behind a plant but I don't think he was a plant, Dulcie."

Dulcie laughed. "Oh! Dot, you are behind the times dear. You know — somebody planted in the crowd to heckle, like they do for comedians. Maybe to keep him on track."

"That was Dave Meldrum," said Frank. "I recognised the voice. He tries to keep a low profile."

"Ha! Fits just nicely behind a potted palm! Just made Longley look more of an idiot than usual! Ah, well. A wedding on Saturday, eh! How did your lunch with Stella go, by the way?" Dottie saw her friend's troubled face. "Oh! Debrief? My joint?"

Dulcie looked at Frank who nodded and smiled. "You go ahead, darling, it'll do you good. I'll see you a bit later. Let's have dinner at seven shall we? We also have a wedding to plan."

"Yes, we do. Thank you, my love. Until then." Dulcie kissed him on the cheek and held his hand a few extra seconds.

The Teapots made tea in Dottie and Dee's room. They sat with their mugs and nibbled ginger nuts.

Dulcie recounted the lunch, crying her way through the last part of the story. Dottie and Dierdre cried with her.

They blew their noses, harrumphed a great deal and then got the notepad out.

"What are we doing to do?" Dottie said, her pile of tissues almost as large as Dulcie's.

"Nothing, I think. We'll just get our wedding organised for the first month we're back at Rosehill and hope she comes. I'll email her tomorrow and apologise, but how can I apologise for the greatest gift of my life? Well, the two greatest gifts, firstly her of course, and then having Frank back. I'm not sure she'll ever understand."

Dee blew her nose again. "Well, girls, we still have some mysteries to unravel — just to keep us busy. Where is Prudence? Where are Joan and Samuel? That idiot major obviously doesn't know that Prudence tried to kill Joan, but he probably knows that it wasn't Sarah. Does he know that Joan set the fire and nearly killed Sarah and wanted to kill you and Frank?"

Dottie chuckled. "You do have a way of putting your finger on the pulse sometimes, don't you, Deeds? The Teapots Gang, that's who we are and it's time we got back to work."

They stood for a hug, laughed and hugged again.

Chapter 19

'I say let the world go to hell,
but I should always have my tea.'
Fyodor Dostoevsky

Saturday dawned grey and cloudy, rain was forecast. Not ideal for a wedding but what could one do, no one had yet figured out how to control the weather.

The erstwhile residents of Rosehill were in a state, they had all shopped for outfits, been to the hairdressers, had their toenails polished, and brushed their dentures, but they still didn't know who was getting married. Secret squirrels it might be, but what if it was someone dull like the major — they would die of boredom and be furious at the expense.

Dulcie and Frank were dispirited and disinterested, but such was the tedium at The Green Ant Hostel that they had girded their loins and put on a brave face. In any case, they were determined to enjoy a drink at somebody else's expense. They'd not heard a word from Stella — no reply to Dulcie's repeated phone calls or emails.

Dulcie remembered how her parents had disowned her when she'd defied them by changing university degrees and falling in love with Frank over fifty years earlier. Now her own daughter was doing the same — and there was nothing she could do about it. They got on with making their plans for their own wedding without knowing when it would be and who might be there. Major Longley insisted that Rosehill would be ready by August; a spring ceremony in September could be held in a marquee on the lawn and the kitchen would be up and running to cater for the guests.

But, for the time being it was someone else's wedding that beckoned. Dulcie was dressed in a pale pink dress with blue periwinkles that matched her eyes, and Frank looked handsome in a grey shirt and blue trews.

The Green Ant's pool was decorated with peach bows on chairs and festoons on pergolas. A timber arbour was draped with white netting and peach satin bows. A table was set at the rear with two chairs behind, a large registry book open on the white cloth.

Major Longley, dressed in his military uniform, looked official and important. There was no sign of the wedding party. Waiters offered glasses of champagne and orange juice, but mostly straight orange juice — didn't want the oldies getting pissed too soon.

A trumpet sounded, then someone switched on an iPod and '*Here comes the bride*' blasted the eardrums of those who were too close to the speakers. They swivelled as one, craning their necks to see who would be coming up the makeshift aisle.

A gasp went up followed by a murmur of surprise, and a small bout of clapping broke out.

"Good God! It can't be." Dulcie nearly choked on a canapé.

"It is though. Bloody hell, what does she look like?" Dee gawped.

"An apricot blancmange, to my way of thinking!" said Dot.

Major Longley coughed and the throng turned their attention to the arbour where Mike Partridge stood, statue-still. He was dressed in a black tuxedo, and a peach satin cummerbund that was stretched to breaking across his tummy.

Prudence, decked out in a matching peach satin creation that looked like it had been copied from something Princess Diana had once worn, limped gamely up the aisle on Dr Prince's arm. Titters punctuated the stunned silence as Prudence's trout mouth turned upwards in a smile as she approached her intended.

Longley opened his mouth to commence the ceremony; his hands were shaking as he held his book of words — the marriage vows.

"Dearly beloved, we are gathered here to witness the marriage between Michael James Partridge and Prudence Felicity De Casembroot.

"What? I didn't know she had a posh name like that, did you?" whispered Dottie to Dulcie.

"No! Ssh!"

Longley continued with the introduction. He took so long over it that the crowd began to fidget, itching to sit down and have a drink. Where was the man behind the palm tree to tell him to get on with it?

At last he intoned: "Do you Michael James Partridge being of sound mind and body, take this woman Prudence Felicity De Casembroot to be your lawful wedded wife, to have and to hold from this day forward, in sickness and in health, for richer or poorer, till death do you part?"

"I do."

"Not sure about the sound mind," giggled Dottie.

"And do you, Prudence Felicity De Casembroot, being of sound mind and body, take this man, Michael James Partridge, to be your lawful wedded husband, to have and to hold from this day forward, in sickness and in health, for richer or poorer, till death do you part?"

"I d…"

A screech of tyres, a blaring of horns and cries of hurray and hurrah interrupted the ceremony. Hoots of laughter accompanied whistles, Christmas trumpets, and drums that split the air. All heads turned to the ruckus.

A collective gasp peppered the crowd. Joan Holloway-Potts-Jones, resplendent in an ivory satin gown, white satin shoes, and a white cloche hat spiked with bird of paradise feathers perched on her newly-coiffed black bob, rode up the aisle in a golf cart with Samuel, clad in full morning dress, sitting on her lap.

"Hellooo! Hellooo! If there's to be a wedding, why not two — a double whammy? Hurrah, my fellow Rosehillians. We're all here together again in spite of all our terrible experiences."

She lifted Samuel off her knees, alighted from the golf cart, strode up to the arbour and addressed Major Longley.

"Pray continue Major. We're here!"

"Joan, I…"

Prudence turned beetroot, threw her little posy over her head and flew at Joan, peach claws bared.

"You fucking bitch. You're not going to spoil my wedding day. You have ruined my life for the last ten years, you have stolen the one man I loved, just because you could, but this is MY wedding day. MINE, do you hear? And you will not spoil it. You will never spoil anything again. I didn't get you last time but I will this time." And she barrelled into Joan until they both teetered on the edge of the pool.

Collective breaths were held. Dulcie caught the posy in one hand and whispered, "Go on Prudence. Push her in."

So she did. Joan went cartwheeling into the pool, Samuel jumped in after her and the crowd went berserk.

Dee giggled. "Did you hear what Prudence said? Didn't get you last time! Huh! A confession! We heard it, didn't we girls?"

Joan came up for air, black wig straining to get away. Samuel bobbed up beside her and tried to get her head into a rescue hold. She swatted him on the noodle and he went under again, bubbles rising to the surface. Prudence, seeing Sam in strife, jumped into the pool and dropped like a greased brick in her heavy peach satin. She surfaced with a gasp and grabbed Samuel's jacket pulling him to the side. Joan was going under repeatedly, her ivory satin dragging her into the deep end.

"I've rescued her once from a swimming pool, I'm not doing it again." Frank chortled and Dulcie nudged him in the side.

Mike threw off his jacket and dived in. He dragged her,

coughing and spluttering to the side, just as Prudence lugged a bedraggled Samuel up the concrete steps. The four lay like vegetables on the edge and applause broke out amongst the onlookers.

'Well, now, there's a wedding for you. Nothing like ours was it," said Mrs. Stillwell, leaning against her husband.

"Did she say 'I do'? I don't think she did. They're not properly married yet," said Mr Stillwell.

The major approached the sodden quartet, his book still clasped in his shaking hands.

"Prudence, you need to say 'I do', so I can pronounce you man and wife."

"Oh, all right. I do. I suppose, I bloody do!" Prudence nodded her sopping head, but her heart wasn't in it.

"I now pronounce you man and wi.."

Prudence was not to be silenced by mere marriage ceremony protocol. "I know you started that fire, Joan. You nearly killed Sarah, you mad cow. I'll make sure you suffer for that and for everything you did to Frank and Dulcie."

"You think … you've won … you stupid little woman," Joan puffed, "you can't beat me, you never could, and never will. And I will have the last laugh. You'll see."

Chapter 20

'Tea to the English is really a picnic indoors.'
Alice Walker

Five Months Later

The marquee shone in the warm September light. Circular tables and chairs for eight were set in front of a small rectangular table that had been placed on a low platform. Waiters and waitresses in black trousers and white short-sleeved shirts bustled to and fro, laying the cutlery and plates, placing flower decorations and periwinkle blue napkins beside the bread plates. A parquet dance floor was laid in front of the top table and a piano sat to one side. A grey-haired lady dressed in a periwinkle skirt and jacket perched on a piano stool and practiced arpeggios and scales to warm up her fingers.

Cups, saucers, water and champagne glasses dotted the tables. Blue muslin, and yellow and white flower posies festooned the columns that held the marquee up; it was breathtaking.

***

In their newly decorated married quarters, not wallpapered with roses, Dulcie was getting ready. Dottie, dressed in similar garb to Dierdre at the piano, was helping to pin and tuck, press and stretch a lemon yellow dress and jacket that Dulcie had chosen at a non-bridal shop in Cairns Central Shopping Centre. It was simple and elegant, just like Dulcie.

"We always said he'd be lucky to have his room redecorated! Pity it took such a hoo-ha to get it done." Dottie chuckled, a pin between her teeth. "Stay still. You're fidgeting and I'll stick this in you if you're not careful."

"I wonder how he's doing. Do you think he's as nervous as I am? Last night was the first time in months we've been apart and it felt like a lifetime again."

'I'm sure he is. Has Michael arrived yet?"

"Yes, he arrived last night and stayed in one of the new guest rooms. He seems like a nice boy. He's got his kids with him too. They don't look like Frank, of course." Dulcie reached for a tissue and blew her nose.

"Now, you're not going to start again are you, Dulce? You know there's nothing you can do."

"I know, I know. I just wish I hadn't told her when I did, then she'd be here to see us married." She sniffed and blew her nose again.

"Hey, it's nearly time to go, or are you going to be fashionably late? Make him wait?"

"No, of course not. I think we've waited long enough, don't you?"

Dulcie peeked out of the window. Cars were parked along the driveway, and people were chatting on the grass outside the marquee. She didn't know who they were but as she and Frank had invited everyone from the home and their families, all the staff and their families too, it was unlikely that she'd know anyone, except for the Teapots, of course … and her beloved man.

"Right, let's get to it then. Look there's Frank with Dr Prince. Oh, he does look handsome in his uniform. Is that a medal on his jacket, Dulce?"

"Yes, he got the Victoria Cross for valour in Vietnam. He saved a lot of soldiers in spite of being badly wounded himself." She sniffed.

"Well I never," said Dottie. "Things you don't know about someone, eh?"

"He doesn't like talking about it." Dulcie hugged her, checked herself in the mirror for the last time, and took her hand.

Frank disappeared into the marquee and the guests followed him in, taking their seats in readiness for the ceremony.

Major Longley ran towards the marquee, late apparently, looking spruce in his formal military uniform, a line of medals glinting in the sun.

Dulcie and Dottie made their way down to the entrance hall of the home. There, Madge and Pamela joined them, both dressed in the same periwinkle suits as Dottie and Dee.

Madge passed Dulcie a little posy, a tiny version of the arrangements in the marquee. She took a deep breath and the small entourage made its way down the steps to the tent entrance.

Dierdre, receiving a nod from Dr Prince, played the opening bars of *Here Comes the Bride.* Mike Partridge popped up from the rear of the marquee and took Dulcie's arm.

Mike patted her hand and they walked sedately up the aisle between the tables.

The onlookers gasped. Dulcie looked radiant, as radiant as any seventy-two year old could be, for it was her birthday as well as her wedding day.

She joined Frank in front of Major Longley. Frank automatically drew himself up as if at attention.

The Major began, his hand steady on his clipboard, where the marriage script was fixed with four strips of extra strong Sellotape.

"Dearly beloved, we are gathered here today to witness the marriage of our very own Dulcie Cassandra Dooley, née Thomson and Frank Chambers."

"Get on with it…!" A voice shouted from behind a potted palm and everyone burst out laughing.

"Quiet in the stalls please — this one, I'll do in my own time."

"It's been a long road to travel for these two people — over fifty years ago they met, losing each other to a war and an inefficient postal service…" Chuckles rippled through the gathering. "But today we celebrate a couple of landmarks — not only this wonderful wedding, but also Dulcie's birthday. Happy Birthday, Dulcie — and, a surprise…"

"That's three things not a couple …" Joyful laughter followed the familiar refrain.

"Ha! Ha! I know," said Longley, "but this one's my special gift to the happy couple."

Dulcie and Frank glanced at each other.

"Yes? All ready?" The major nodded at Dierdre who keyed the opening bars of '*I'll always love you*' and a pure sweet voice began to sing.

Dulcie whirled around. Standing at the entrance, flanked by Bart, and their children was Stella, her voice flying to the roof of the tent as she sang the chorus of the Whitney Houston hit.

Dulcie gaped at Frank and they were about to rush down the aisle when Stella began walking towards them. As she finished the final bar she came to stand in front of her mother. Dulcie opened her arms and her daughter fell into them, tears pouring down her cheeks.

"I'm so sorry, Mum."

"Nothing to be sorry about, darling. You're here now. We all are." Dulcie reached for Frank who came into the embrace, looked into his daughter's eyes and kissed her cheek.

"Any chance we can finish this ceremony then?" Longley interrupted.

Dottie passed Dulcie a tissue and stepped to one side to let Stella stand beside her mother and father.

Longley continued with the marriage vows and all too soon reached the most important part.

"Do you Frank Chambers take this woman Dulcie Cassandra Dooley née Thomson — oh, etcetera etcetera, to be your wife — at last?"

"I most definitely do," chuckled Frank.

"And Dulcie, do you do the same? With him?"

"Oh yes, Major, I certainly do!"

"Phew! Good, then in that case, by the power invested in me…"

"Get on with it, for Gawd's sake …" and the guests erupted.

"I now pronounce you — husband and wife!"

THE END

ABOUT THE AUTHOR

Gabi is primarily an editor but as a seasoned editor she made sure this book was professionally edited by someone else.

I would like to thank my dear friend Jo Anne Cracknell for her excellent work in putting my errors to rights.

I wrote this book in 2016 as part of a Trilogy. The second one is half way written and, if all things are equal during this crazy lockdown time around the world, I might actually get the second and third book written.

Thank you for reading Frank and Dulcie's story.

Any comments please sent to gabiplumm@bigpond.com or perhaps write a little review on my book page: https://www.amazon.com/gp/product/B08J74JDCY/ref=dbs_a_def_rwt_bibl_vppi_i0

Milton Keynes UK
Ingram Content Group UK Ltd.
UKHW021557110124
435868UK00009B/707

9 780646 826974